THE DAWN PATROL

A NAME WIPED OFF, WHOSE NEXT INSCRIBING WILL BE
UPON A TABLET OF BRONZE.

THE
DAWN PATROL

NOVELIZED BY
GUY FOWLER

FROM THE FIRST NATIONAL
AND VITAPHONE PICTURE

STARRING

RICHARD BARTHELMESS

DIRECTED BY HOWARD HAWKS
AND BASED ON AN ORIGINAL
STORY BY JOHN MONK SAUNDERS

ILLUSTRATED WITH SCENES
FROM THE PHOTOPLAY

GROSSET & DUNLAP
PUBLISHERS   NEW YORK

To DICK BARTHELMESS . . .

What I might say in praise of him
would be, in a manner of speaking,
like shipping oranges to California
. . . and with a gesture of appreciation to John Monk Saunders who con-
ceived for him the perfect rôle—the
rôle of a *man*.

—G.F.

*If I should die, think only
this of me,
That there's some corner of
a foreign soil
That is forever England.*
—RUPERT BROOKE

THE DAWN PATROL

CHAPTER I

IN ALL that he ever did Dick Courtney went
the limit. His life was like that. When he
gambled the stakes were high. He played to
win, but he could also stand defeat. In the
single love that swept into his life there was a
lasting passion. In a word, Courtney was in-
tense.

Some of us can approach the flame and escape with a mere scorching. But those rare
men of Courtney's sort go plunging into the
crucible of white heat that is life at its peak.
They recognize no middle ground. They rise
to the heights, or go down to oblivion with the
failure of their hopes, flaming meteors that
fall and are extinguished.

It was inevitable that Courtney should come
eventually to the First Combat Group, just as
it was logical for a man of his type to love Lady
Mary Cambridge back in London. In fact, it
was the very hopelessness of his passion that
brought him down into the cathedral pines of

1

Allonville Forest when England was facing her doom. They particularly needed men who held no brief for life.

He came with a reckless laugh on his lips, but his eyes were haunted. Camel Squadron 31 was shattered, yet the remnants were flinging ironic jests as they drank raw brandy, or whisky and soda at the improvised squadron bar that night.

It was in February of 1916. The German offensive against Verdun was just beginning. Down in Gallipoli the British and French troops had been withdrawn a month earlier and the Austrians already occupied Montenegro. An atmosphere of fatalism hung over the Western Front like the brooding battle smoke. It was a time when Englishmen believed secretly that Britain was defeated.

At first Dick Courtney's name was mentioned only in a rumor. Even then it was a name to stir vague emotions, for his fantastic career in the Royal Air Force had already set him apart. The word drifted into the bar that Courtney was coming in as a replacement.

"Along with a few cadets to crack up the few ships we've got left," remarked Roger Willoughby.

"Courtney." The name came softly on the

lips of Rex Parker, whose face, but for his prematurely aged eyes, was that of a boy.

"An odd beggar," he mused. "They say the devil doesn't want him——"

"For fear he'd raise hell," Willoughby suggested.

Parker shrugged and drained a tumbler of brandy. His hard blue eyes were set in bloodshot rims that gave him a weird expression.

"Destiny," he drawled, "has a way of dealing the aces. God knows we've been dealt enough jokers."

Willoughby nodded.

"Fancy Courtney in this," he gazed about him at the group of fliers. "He and Major Brand will never hit it off. Courtney won't stand for discipline—even such as we have here."

"He'll scarcely need to—if he can bring down Fokkers."

Willoughby chuckled and refilled his glass.

"Discipline be damned," he raised the glass. "And God bless Courtney."

They drank and turned the talk to other channels, but elsewhere in the smoke-filled quarters the rumor carried on. Behind the bar Roy Crandall, mixing endless drinks, heard Courtney's name repeatedly.

"I say," he interrupted a group of pilots, "this Courtney, now, is he a drinking man, what?"

A fleeting silence fell upon them. They faced him solemnly across the bar. Young Webley-Wentworth who would come into a title if he lived, smiled lazily.

"Crandall, old man, your ignorance is appalling."

He leaned upon the bar confidentially.

"In a dog fight not long ago," he resumed, "Courtney's Lewis gun jammed. Now listen to me, Crandall, here's what he did, so help me. He leaned out of the cockpit as he zoomed up on a Fokker—he blew his breath—hard, you understand—and the damned Heinie burst into flames."

Crisp staccato laughter rippled among the hearers and Crandall joined. He indicated with a sweeping gesture the rude signs that were posted on the walls naming the favorite squadron drinks. There was the Gangrene Cocktail and the Mamie Taylor, the Open Pore and the Angel's Teat, the Major Bailey and Planter's Punch.

"I'll work up a Courtney Cocktail," he promised gayly.

"Good," exclaimed Webley-Wentworth.

"Give it a petrol base, old dear, with a dash of liquid TNT."

Thus they laughed through the night, forgetful of yesterday's holocaust, heedless of tomorrow's dawn. Boys, most of them, intent on making each moment count, dulling their senses in alcohol that they might not count the moments.

In view of the facts they couldn't be blamed. It was no secret that the squadron had been picked for the sacrifice. No flight went out with its seven droning planes that ever came back whole. But the British command had no choice. It stiffened up the lines when a flight passed over. The infantrymen knew then that the air was patrolled.

So it was that Squadron 31 celebrated each night the return of its lambs who escaped the slaughter, and with sardonic humor drank to those who would fly out when morning came. They laughed and sang with their drinking, but they never discussed defeat. A missing pilot was not defeated, but merely a victim of bad luck.

That first rumor about Courtney was verified promptly with the arrival of Major Drake Brand. He swung into the room and there was a fleeting halt in the laughter that came with a subtle change in the atmosphere of relaxation. Even when he nodded curtly and called for whisky and soda there was still a tensity, as though they were uneasy in his presence.

A raucous gramophone with a perpetually faulty needle was playing "Poor Butterfly."

"Shut the damned thing off," snapped someone.

Until Brand's arrival the music had gone on unnoticed. He sipped his drink. He was young like the rest of them, but his face was lined. He had tired eyes. The talk resumed all around him, but there was an odd new note of subdued gayety that was somehow not quite spontaneous and free. The explanation, of course, was simple enough. Brand had set himself up as a disciplinarian of sorts, and in theory the men were with him. The subject had been drummed into them enough as cadets, but that was before the winter of 1916 . . . before they knew so precisely how a living laugh could become a death's-head grin in the brief sputter of a Vickers gun ten thousand feet aloft.

Major Brand set down his glass and turned to Lieutenant Webley-Wentworth, who happened to be nearest.

"I've had rather good news."

The lieutenant arched his eyebrows and waited curiously.

"G.H.Q. advises me that Captain Courtney is joining us to-night."

Wentworth affected surprise. It would not be diplomatic, he knew, to say that the news had already drifted out from the orderly room.

"Courtney," he exclaimed. "Gad, Major, we're in luck."

Brand studied the contents of his glass, and his eyes were clouded.

"Quite so," he said at length, "but I hope what I hear of him isn't altogether true."

His subordinate remained courteously silent. Curious eyes were turned on them but no one interrupted. The general conversation resumed and again the gramophone began to grind out cracked melody.

"Courtney," said the major, "notoriously doesn't care a damn for orders. He's a lonely pirate, I've heard—likes to pop off by himself and see what turns up. He's a miracle, of course, but—well, up here on this line we've got to hang together, y'see. It's damned imperative."

Wentworth nodded thoughtfully. The major frowned.

"What's more," he added, "I gather that Courtney takes his rum neat—and in large doses."

His companion chuckled.

"Don't we all, Major?"

Brand permitted himself a frosty smile.

"Too damn much, young man, entirely too much."

Wentworth shrugged.

"One must do something," he ventured.

Brand observed him steadily, and for a swift instant his granite face softened.

"I suppose you're right, Lieutenant. But it isn't good, just the same. A man needs a clear head for this business."

Wentworth shrugged expressively.

"Perhaps," he conceded, "but for myself, Major, I don't want to think too much. None of us does, y'know. After all, it's mechanical. You shove off, or you limp home—it all depends on the way you kick the bus about."

Brand finished his drink and declined another.

"When Courtney reports," he suggested, "I hope he gets the impression that we fly in formation. I'll tell him, of course, but when he trickles in on you here, you might talk about it, Lieutenant."

Wentworth laughed.

"Kind of you, Major, to assume that I might influence him."

Brand hesitated.

"G.H.Q. gave me Courtney," he murmured,

"in response to my urgent request for veteran pilots. They're sending some cadets, three I believe. I prefer to induce Courtney to see this my way rather than to be harsh."

His cold steady eyes met Wentworth's and suddenly they were glittering with something almost savage.

"Squadron 31," he snapped, "obeys orders. I want that passed about, Lieutenant, before I put the screws on. Y'understand?"

Wentworth was lazily amused, but his reply was respectful.

"Very well, sir. I'll do what I can."

Major Brandon wheeled, and as he passed from the room he nodded a curt good-night that swept them all.

Wentworth found Parker beside him. He nodded abruptly.

"The war is about to begin in earnest, old dear," he drawled.

*   *   *   *   *   *   *

It was after midnight when Courtney arrived from Paris in a motorcycle side car. He had been on forty-eight-hour leave and very drunk. He climbed from the cramped machine stiffly and nodded to the sentry.

"Captain Courtney reporting." He spoke huskily. "My compliments to Major Brand."

"Yes, sir. Major Brand left word for you, Captain. Your quarters are ready, sir. He'll see you in the morning."

Courtney nodded in the thick night.

"Good. Where do I get a slug?"

"You'll find the bar in the officers' quarters, Captain."

Courtney nodded and faced the mud-spattered man who had driven him down. He smiled and there was a chuckle in his voice.

"Nice ride, Simpkins. Thanks."

He pressed a note into the man's hand and turned away.

"Lor' bless me, sir," the driver bent low to study the money, "you've 'anded me five pounds, you 'ave, sir."

Courtney laughed.

"It's good Bank of England stuff, Simpkins."

He strode away toward the squat quarters where a handful of hard-drinking pilots still lingered. They looked up quickly as the travel-stained stranger paused in the doorway. He was tall and gaunt, but his lips were curled in a curious smile as he saw them.

"The dawn patrol," he said quietly, "guarding our most precious supplies."

Crandall, who had come from behind the bar

to sit at a round table in early morning familiarity with the others, sprang to his feet.

"Captain Courtney. Welcome, sir, an' what'll you have?"

The others rose languidly and with easy cordiality greeted him. Wentworth was there, along with Parker and a trio of replacements less than a week in the squadron. Courtney twisted out of his coat and tossed it in a corner. His uniform, except for the field boots, was unstained and trim.

"A spot of brandy, if you don't mind." He swept the group with a glance from peculiarly burning eyes. "Gentlemen, may I have the pleasure?"

He dropped easily into a chair and was one of them.

"Paris?" asked Wentworth, equally complacent.

Courtney laughed. It was a paradox of sound, for it was pleasantly mellow, yet with a note of irony that was without humor.

"Paris," he repeated, "on forty-eight hours' leave."

"Women?" Wentworth's laconic question was put as though he anticipated the answer.

Courtney shrugged.

"No, my weakness is whisky."

Parker chuckled.

"Gad, you're fortunate to have but one, old man."

"I make that one count," Courtney told him.

His expression was pleasant enough, but there was in his tone a note that suggested the contact of metal. A queer silence hung over them for an instant. It was one of those pregnant atoms of time in which men weigh one another and subconsciously form their judgments.

Wentworth was the first to speak.

"What do you hear up the line, Captain?"

It was as though he were asking for gossip from London. Courtney tossed off three fingers of brandy and reached for the bottle which Crandall had set conveniently before him. He poured the liquid slowly and held the glass up between his critical eye and the light.

"They're giving us the scotching of our lives," he said casually.

"All along the front?"

Courtney nodded.

"It's like any other gamble." He lowered his peculiar eyes to gaze at the tip of his boot. "If the odds run against you and you stay with it long enough, the odds change."

He suddenly laughed and now, instead of

draining the glass, he sipped at the fiery liquor as though it were a cordial.

"I say, they tell me your major is a martinet —strong on red tape—that sort of thing. Is that true?"

Wentworth fingered his glass thoughtfully.

"He's rather keen for discipline."

"I understand." Courtney's smile was bitterly sardonic. "Brass-hat stuff, eh?"

The others laughed.

"Something of the sort," Wentworth agreed. "He's set against solo work, Courtney."

"So I've been told."

"Y'see," Parker suggested, "we're so damned close-up here that Major Brand counts more on morale than records. I mean to say, he'd rather keep the squadron working over the lines than hang up a lot of ribbons. But even at that, we can't keep a flight in one piece more than a day or two."

Courtney nodded his understanding.

"The major's right, no doubt. I'll never question him. But the only kick I get out of this show is killing Germans."

"We do that on occasion," Wentworth said dryly.

Courtney's laugh was sincere and for the first time real warmth came into his eyes.

"Well put, Wentworth. I deserved it. But I didn't mean what I said in the way you took it, old man. Y'see, I've never been in doubt that I'm at fault. I've been ragged by more G.H.Q. stiffnecks than you've fingers and toes. And they were right. But the fact is, when I see a chance I have to bolt after it. I can't help myself."

There was something humble in the way he spoke, almost an apology. It broke the lingering strain in the atmosphere and at once gave them an understanding of the man, without which there would have been a wall between them forever. When a strange god grows humble those who have worshiped him from afar grow to love him even more. It was so with Courtney now. Wentworth spoke impulsively.

"Of course, Captain, I understand. We all do. I envy you."

Courtney observed him levelly.

"It's my curse." He laughed shortly. "I'll go to hell—when I'm not sent. But otherwise—" he shrugged and his laugh was oddly boyish.

"I've been lucky—devilish lucky," he added.

Wentworth indicated the youngsters, scarcely younger than himself in fact, but lacking his experience in action.

"You'll be putting bad ideas in their heads, Captain. We're all living on superstition up here now. We've a black cat for a mascot. Fact is, we're living on luck—or the hope of it."

Courtney raised his glass.

"May the luck hold out and the black cat have nine kittens!"

Parker soberly shook his head in the negative.

"No, Captain," he drawled, "he'll never do that."

They drank and the youngest of the replacements glanced at his wrist watch. He was a fresh-cheeked lad named Cheyney.

"I'm off," he announced. "Two hours of shut-eye and we hop. Good night, Captain."

Courtney rose and took his hand.

"Hope to be with you, old man. Anyway, bon voyage."

Cheyney flushed, struggling to be nonchalant.

"Thanks, sir. We'll be looking for you."

Presently, Crandall went to his quarters with a final warning flung over his shoulders.

"You can't drink it all up before daylight."

Courtney waved his slim powerful hand in a friendly gesture.

"Very well, Crandall. We'll do our damnedest anyway."

He turned to Parker and Wentworth.

"Are you on the list this morning?" His tone was mildly curious.

Parker was showing his liquor. He wagged his head wearily.

"On to-day an' off t'morrow," he muttered. "Now I'm a rooster 'n' t'morrow I'll be a feather duster."

Courtney became solicitous.

"Really, old man, I'm sorry I've been keeping you up. You fellows turn in. I'll take a bottle along and check into my quarters."

Parked eyed him owlishly.

"Y'mean, Cap'n, you're goin' t' drink s'more?"

Courtney studied him, only half smiling.

"I keep it around for company," he admitted. "If I don't sleep well, y'know, I like to have a little spot beside my cot."

Parker nodded.

"Wonderful," he announced. " 'Pon my word, ol' man, I don't know where you put it."

He leaned over the table confidentially.

"Tell you what t' do, Courtney, with a tank like yours." He tapped the table with a stiffened forefinger. "Fill 'er up an' t' hell with everything. If I didn't always get drunk I could drink more——"

Wentworth lowered one eye in signal to

Courtney and took his friend by the arm.
"All right, Rex. The sandman's coming now.
Ready—one—two—three."

He drew Parker to his feet and started toward the door. Courtney took the bottle, picked up his trench coat and followed them. Outside he ranged beside Parker and assisted Wentworth with the dragging pilot between them.

"He'll be on the line at dawn fresh as a daisy," Wentworth told him.

Courtney nodded.

"Youth," he muttered. "You can't drug it."

In the darkness Wentworth turned a penetrating glance upon him and was silent. Courtney walked steadily erect. He had drunk more than any of them. But for a dark flush on his bronzed cheeks and a strange glowing fire in his eyes, there was no outward effect.

"Your quarters are in there."

Wentworth indicated the place.

"Mine are just beyond. I'll cover this up."
He indicated Parker who was walking in his sleep. "If he howls in the night fire a couple of shots through his door."

Courtney smiled.

"Noise never disturbs me, Lieutenant. Good night."

"Good night."

Courtney found his luggage on the floor where an orderly had left it. He flung off his uniform and from the little trunk drew out a faded dressing gown. He felt in the pocket for a very old-looking briar and stuffed it with tobacco from a pouch. On the table he placed the bottle, still half full of brandy, then kneeled over his kit. Without disturbing the contents appreciably he found with sure hand an oblong flat parcel.

He removed the cord carefully and next the paper wrapping. At length he withdrew a portrait in a handsome silver frame. He set it precisely in the center of the table where the meager light would fall upon the picture. It was the face of a singularly lovely girl. Thrust into the frame was a card which bore in a fine hand a brief verse——

To every man there openeth a Way
 And Ways and a Way,
And the High Soul climbs the High Way
 And the Low Soul gropes the Low,
And in between, on the misty flats the rest
  drift to and fro.
But to every man there openeth a High Way
  and a Low,
And every man decideth the Way his soul
  shall go.

Courtney's lips twisted in a bitter grimace. He remembered every quality of her voice when Mary Cambridge had quoted that stanza by John Oxenham. He stood gazing down into the calm face that looked back at him now no less steadily than she had done that night at Cambridge Towers. . . .

"I'm fond of you, Dick—awfully fond of you. But I don't love you because I don't respect you as I should."

There had been no bitterness. On the contrary, her voice trembled and her eyes were soft with an emotion that she was too honest to even try to hide. He recalled his laconic question.

"Why?"

"Because," she had told him steadily, "you don't respect yourself."

Courtney continued to study the portrait as he filled a tumbler from the bottle. He drained it at a gulp and set it down.

"You were quite right, Mary," he muttered. "I don't."

CHAPTER II

HE STOOD there for another moment observing the inanimate beauty of the picture with brooding eyes. Suddenly he shrugged and turned to the stiffly uncomfortable rocking-chair that complained in all its ancient joints when he sat down. He lit the pipe slowly, careful to touch the flame to the whole surface of the tobacco. This deliberate manner was somehow incongruous, yet here alone in his quarters there could be no motive for a pose.

Courtney smiled oddly at his own situation. He sprawled in the low-seated chair with his long legs stretched out before him, his shoulders hunched. In the dim glow of the wall light his face was drawn in somber relief so that the lines were deeply shadowed. His dark crisp hair was disordered. He smoked with the infrequent languid inhalations of a man who understands his pipe. The lazy smoke spiraled over his bowed head and drifted like incense to the gods of night.

This, he told himself, was the beginning of a new adventure. He did not concern himself with its ending, or with the possibility of the next one. Courtney had ceased long ago to look for anything new in fighting. He had, to his way of thinking, lost the very thrill of life in his bitter indifference to death.

Just once he raised his head to gaze from narrowed eyes at the portrait of Lady Mary. His face was expressionless. But his brain recoiled at memories and stubbornly, with subconscious tenacity, turned to the hateful process of self-analysis. He could never avoid that, even when he drank. It was Courtney's curse to know himself. He was devoting his energies to forget the knowledge, but all that he did was futile.

He knew, in that moment of poignant introspection, as he had always known, that every fiber of his being called out for the solid things of life . . . home and old associations, books and tranquil hours, children . . . most of all, children. He knew the worth of old and trusted friends, the value of traditions, and the comfort of decency. He thought, too, that he could vision the glory of love.

But as these things ran through his mind Courtney's face underwent a transformation. Where his deep sullen eyes had been quiet they flamed. Lines in his jaws that had been soft in an expression of gentle humor grew harsh and deep. The tranquil smile that had lingered briefly on his lips became a leer. He became suddenly the fiend that enemy airmen knew, the killer whose relentless pursuit was feared the more because of his devilish lack of caution.

He jerked to his feet and lurched toward the table. With trembling hands he poured from the bottle into the tumbler and held it in a gesture to the portrait.

"And every man decideth which way his soul shall go." He quoted that final line of the verse and his voice was harsh. He emptied the glass and set it down. His short laugh was full of anguish.

"That is a lie." He stared madly at the calm-eyed portrait as though he expected it to answer him. "A damned unfair lie, Mary."

He sank back into the chair and glanced at his wrist watch. Dawn was yet two hours away. He knew that it would be useless to try to sleep. That came only when he returned from a patrol utterly weary, nearing the limit of physical endurance. Then he could sleep. As a man sleeps who sinks into the stupor of a powerful drug. The brain had to quit first. After that the body surrendered. But never before.

Now, with the brandy burning his throat, seemingly flowing with the blood in his veins, he could be calm again for a time. He could bear the self-inflicted torture of remembering. He took an almost fiendish delight in thus living again through scenes that caused him mental agony. . . .

He sat with his eyes fixed steadily on the picture in the silver frame. She wore that same expression the night at Cambridge Towers when he had last seen her . . . two years ago, little short of three now. . . . God, could it be possible? That was in June before the little tongue of flame at Sarajevo became a fiery inferno that enveloped Europe.

In August he had joined his regiment and a fortnight later landed in France . . . the swift transition from infantry to air force . . . cadet days when Navarre and Nungesser, Ball and Bishop were gods . . . then his own baptism high over the lines and the strange realization that death didn't matter. Even then he had hoped in his rare moments of optimism that her decision was not irrevocable.

It was in Paris that he first heard the truth. He stirred uneasily and his glittering eyes lingered on the brandy that was almost gone . . . the recollection forced itself keenly upon him.

Back in London Lady Mary was flinging herself into war work.

"She's going about with young——"

A pink-cheeked lieutenant had started to tell him.

"Damn you, keep it to yourself."

Courtney remembered his savage fury, the startled face of the boy, his muttered apology. But indirectly, from the sources that filtered news from London to the lines, he had gradually heard the rest of it . . . all except the name.

He had succeeded in withholding that last thrust from his tortured brain. He knew even now only that the other man was Oxford, wealthy, of good breeding and was somewhere in the service, of course. And that Mary Cambridge loved him.

He rose and took the picture from the table. He wrapped it again and bound it. He had done this each night through two years of hell. The man, whoever he might be, would never find the portrait of Lady Mary in Courtney's quarters. At first he had carried the thing along in a DeHaviland scout, but he quit that practice. It was too risky.

He replaced it carefully in his bag and went back to the table. His smile was bitterly sardonic as he lifted the bottle up before the light to study its dwindling contents. This time when he filled the glass it left the bottle empty.

He tossed the drink down in a gulp and flung himself on the cot with a last study of his watch. He had an hour to wait. . . .

For fifteen minutes he lay motionless, his eyes wide open. Rising, he prepared a bath in his quaint collapsible tub and refreshed, carefully shaved himself before a hand mirror. He put on a pair of fresh boots, brushed his uniform and eased his heavy shoulders into the leather harness of his equipment. Shortly before dawn he strode into the mess room, where half a dozen pilots were drinking hot black coffee. Most of them were haggard and drawn. Courtney was peculiarly clear-eyed and fit.

Lieutenant Webley-Wentworth was the first to greet him.

"I say, Captain," he stared blandly, "you must be twins. It's never the same man who left me three hours ago."

Courtney laughed.

"Yes, thank God there's only one of me, Wentworth."

He saw the men stiffen and followed their gaze to the door. Major Brand was there, alert and nervous. Courtney saluted and stood at attention.

"Ah, Captain, you came in late." Brand touched his cap.

"After midnight, sir."

"Good. Glad you're with us. Aren't you up a bit early?"

"I thought you might have an extra crate for me, sir."

The major studied him approvingly and his straight mouth twitched at the corners.

"Not this morning, Courtney. The flight's been posted. Anyway, we're short on ships, damn it. And I want to talk with you before you go out."

Brand accepted the coffee which was handed to him and sipped at it gingerly.

"We're short of everything," he muttered between sips. "Men, too. They've been pegging away at the First Combat outfit all winter, y'know."

Courtney nodded silently. His somber eyes lighted at the sudden burst of a motor tuning up. He walked to the window and gazed into the dim gray mist of morning toward the tarmac. Seven ghostly ships were waiting there. Men moved about them like wraiths. The roar of leashed power came muffled and died down as mechanics played the throttles. When he faced the men again Courtney's expression had hardened and his manner was crisp and brutal.

"You'll be on the line soon, Captain." Major Brand moved up beside him.

"I hope so, Major."

Brand glanced at him curiously and nodded to the others. He led the way across the field. Wentworth continued to talk lightly and the others joined him. Courtney was silent. He walked with his head bowed, frowning at the ground. Parker, who was acting flight commander for the day, was telling a ribald story.

Courtney growled savagely to himself. Schoolboys, he raged inwardly, trying to make a brave show. More afraid of a natural human fear than of death. Seven of them going out, not all to return. In his mind's eye he saw the flight come limping home and he knew in advance that the pilots would be grinning.

An oath ripped from his lips involuntarily. Wentworth touched his arm.

"It's hell to stay home." He spoke in a monotone.

Courtney nodded.

"It isn't altogether that. But I hate the lecture I'll have to swallow."

Wentworth laughed softly.

"Choke it down, old man. Once you're in the air, y'know—" his shoulders moved expressively.

They came up to the Camels and immediately divided, each man climbing eagerly into his own cockpit. Courtney stood beside the major who had his arm raised so that he could study his watch. In the thundering crescendo of the motors all other sounds were lost now. Up in the cockpits human heads had become grotesque leather masks with staring round glass eyes.

Brand swung his arm in an arc. Parker's ship ran out across the field and flung into the wind. As he opened the throttle the second plane sped in his wake. In another instant Parker was pointing up in a steep climb. One by one the others zoomed after him.

They banked into formation presently and headed toward the lighting east. Major Brand was gnawing on his lower lip. He grunted angrily and wheeled.

"It's like that every day," he snapped. "They go out laughing. If they only wouldn't laugh——"

Courtney snarled. His superior officer stared at him.

"Hell, Major," he spoke without the prescribed tone of humility, "they're not bishops. They're boys—afraid to die and hiding it."

Brand looked away.

"I know. I've watched their kind often enough."

They moved together toward the field office.

"Your nerves are on edge, Courtney."

"Not particularly."

They entered the little office in silence. The

major's orderly rose smartly and stood at attention. Inside his private compartment, which was only a frame cell, Brand indicated a chair. He dropped into his own behind the flat desk.

"I suppose you know why G.H.Q. shipped you to us," he began.

Courtney shrugged.

"They told me you were short of men, sir."

"What I lack, Captain, is a flight commander."

Courtney turned a searching gaze into his face.

"I'm no hand at that, sir." He seemed to dismiss the possibility almost as though he were in command and Brand were his inferior in rank.

"No," the major agreed quietly, "you haven't been. But up here you'll get the trick."

Courtney returned his gaze steadily. A peculiar gleam crept into his eyes as he anticipated the instructions.

"Up here," Brand resumed evenly, "there's no roving commission, Captain. We're a combat group, to be sure, but, actually, our most important work is to observe. You've been told that, I believe."

"Something of the sort, sir."

Brand lit a cigarette and pushed the box across the desk.

"We haven't the machinery or the men for solo stuff," he went on casually. "Our whole job right now is to keep the infantry happy. For that reason, Captain——"

Courtney laughed unpleasantly.

"I'm not to break formation."

Brand flushed, but controlled his swift resentment at the interruption.

"Exactly. You're to lead the flight in the morning. I'll expect you to stay with it."

Courtney was silent. His haunted eyes turned to the window and sought the distant sky that was yet gray and drab. The heavy rumble of artillery suddenly came to them distinctly.

"I am aware of your record, Courtney." The major's voice was not without a note of friendly warmth. "G.H.Q. rates you—well, your citations tell you that. But we need morale up here. You've made this war a personal lark and you've been lucky—as well as a first-rate pilot."

Courtney gestured impatiently and forced a smile.

"Thanks, Major. I understand." He rose and stood looking down at his superior. "But I don't fancy it's possible for G.H.Q. to understand. I'm not cut out to be an observation pilot, sir. They won't believe that——"

Brand stood up, too. He smiled soothingly.

"The trouble is, Captain, up till now you've been responsible only for yourself. It wasn't enough. I'm going to hang seven men and seven ships on you. Perhaps a load like that will hold you down."

They faced one another for a moment and a subtle challenge passed between them. Courtney spoke first.

"May I ask a hypothetical question, Major— a point of information?"

"Of course, Captain."

"Presuming that we—the flight is in proper formation and good condition, and I should see an enemy plane looking for trouble, would I be disobeying your orders——"

"You would. You're not to quit the formation, Captain, under any circumstances, except in a dog fight where you're temporarily forced out. Is that clear?"

"Very well, sir."

Courtney saluted mechanically and started to leave. At the door he wheeled.

"Have I your permission to warm up one of the ships, sir? I'd like to get my hand in before the patrol."

Brand studied him sharply.

"That will be all right, Courtney. But stay on our own lines. We can't risk the loss of a spare ship at this stage," he smiled wryly, "not to mention an extra man."

"Thank you, sir."

He moved back to the hangars unhurriedly. Three single-place planes were up on wooden horses while mechanics swarmed over them from props to tail skids. Courtney walked slowly beside the nearest ship and opened an easy conversation with a sergeant mechanic.

"What is the best you can say for the lot, Sergeant?"

The man pointed to the ship in the center.

"That one's about ready, sir. It was Lieutenant Waldron's ship up till yesterday morning."

Courtney strode over to the elevated fuselage and examined it from below.

"Fuel tank hit?"

The sergeant nodded respectfully.

"Waldron brought her home, sir, and went to blighty."

"Bad?"

"Through the head, sir."

Courtney walked around the plane studying it with critical eyes that overlooked nothing. He marked the patches in the wings and sides. Presently he went up on the step and peered down into the office.

"How about the gun?"

A First National Picture. *The Dawn Patrol.*

BEHIND THE ENEMY LINES, A VICTORY OVER INVADING AIRCRAFT HAS ITS PRICE.

"All proper, sir." The sergeant was equally laconic.

"How soon may I have her?"

"If you can give us 'alf an hour, Captain, she'll be ready."

"Fill the tank and put in an extra drum, Sergeant."

"Very well, sir."

Courtney went out and made his way to the bar. He found the usual contingent of idle pilots, too nervous to sleep. He drank raw brandy, while they joined him in highballs. They were a little in awe of him and struggled to conceal the fact, as they tried to accept him casually. He remained twenty minutes and returned to the hangar. The mechanics were pulling the patched ship out to the tarmac.

"We finished up sooner than we expected, Captain." The sergeant greeted him.

It was enough. The sergeant was an understanding soul when it came to pilots and motors. Courtney went lightly up to the cockpit and settled himself. Down at the propeller the sergeant awaited his signal to turn the blade. He raised his arm and reached for the switch. For a few moments he toyed with the throttle, depending upon his ears to test the drone of the power.

Then, with a casual wave over the side, he

sent the little ship into a swift run across the
worn earth. The familiar exultant happiness
that he felt only when he fondled the controls
swept over him now as he climbed. Directly
the field lay beneath him like an oblong patch
in the darker color of the pines. Far below
the left wing tip he could make out the ragged
twisting scar that was the line.

White puffballs appeared intermittently and
in places the earth was hidden beneath a rolling
cloud of sullen smoke. He could hear nothing
above the rhythmic song of his engine. Instinctively he drew the stick back and pointed
up. Whatever else Courtney did he intended
never to get caught in friendly artillery range.
Ten miles up the line he circled over a sector
that was under heavy bombardment.

He kept watching the sky above him and on
every side for the fleeting speck that would be
a wandering fighter from the Jagdstaffel units
of the enemy. For a quarter of an hour he
looped and dived above the lines in the aimless
ecstasy of complete freedom. Straightening
from a spin, his roving eye caught the awk-
ward shape of a distant sausage balloon. He
remembered Brand's instructions.

It occurred to him that if he climbed into the
clouds he might honestly lose his course. He
might dive then. . . .

With luck and not too much conscience, it would bring him out of the cloud banks just above the sausage.

He promptly opened the throttle and pulled the stick far back. The stanch little plane fairly stood on its tail. Down in the filth of the first line the British troops who saw him paused for an instant while their rifles cooled, fascinated by the crazy maneuver. In another instant they lost him.

Courtney bored up through the clouds, watching his instruments. It was guess-work when he straightened off and idled, then gently shoved the stick ahead. He saw the nose drop and felt the rush of wind on his face. It swept against both cheeks with equal pressure so that he knew he was going down in a vertical dive. The wires hummed a taut protest and he felt the ship vibrate beneath the strain.

He shot out from the clouds almost instantly. The wings were glistening wet. In that first running sight of the earth below he glimpsed the balloon. Even as he kicked the rudder to swing around he saw that they were hauling the sausage to the ground on its wavering cable. At the same time the aircraft guns began to speak. He heard a soft explosion not unlike the bursting of a rocket. The plane sagged in a current and off on his right a puff of white smoke appeared like a huge spreading blossom.

Courtney laughed and held the stick down. He leaned over to press his eye against the Aldis sight. The sausage was like the wrinkled ham of a disgusting hog. He tripped the trigger. A burst of tracers spat angrily out through the propeller field. Then, flattening off and for a throbbing instant riding on gravity alone, he sent a current of steel into the flabby belly. Instantly it burst into flame.

He saw the observer climb over the edge of his basket and push himself off into space. Staring over the side, he could see, too, the white faces of men stark against the darkness of their back-tilted helmets. He laughed insanely and pulled the throttle wide.

As the ship responded, Courtney scanned the air about him from force of habit. He knew instinctively that the Vickers guns were spitting steel from below. He would be beyond their range in a minute. At three thousand feet he kicked the rudder to bank over toward the British lines. The same mysterious sense that had served him so many times before came to his rescue now. He twisted about in his place and looked up.

A thousand feet above him and diving, a Checkerboard Fokker was on his tail. Without an instant's pause Courtney shoved the stick forward and went into a power dive. He held it until his instinct told him that to go farther was to crash. He centered the controls gently, feeling the ship. As it straightened out he stared up and saw the Checkerboard riding over him.

Instantly he pulled into a vertical climb, firing as he went up. The startled German kicked over in a roll to avoid a collision. With his faster ship, better equipped and vastly easier to maneuver, he could hold the advantage. But Courtney, with the fierce desperation that had sent his name along the line in an exaggerated legend, headed straight for him with the Lewis spurting yellow flame.

Like all such encounters, it ended in less time than it takes a deliberate man to light his pipe. The Fokker lurched on one wing. Courtney turned loose another burst of steel and climbed. Gazing back over the tail of his ship, he watched the Checkered plane go down.

It fell in a brief oblique, leaving a trail of black smoke. The pilot jumped, but his parachute, trailing above him, became snarled in the undercarriage and he crashed behind the British lines.

Courtney opened the throttle wide and headed for Allonville Forest. He went down in a mild spiral and ran lightly in to the tarmac. His face was darkly flushed and his eyes still glittered with the strange savage light that so frequently disturbed them. As he dropped easily to the ground the mechanics gathered about him at once.

"Nice bus, Sergeant," he remarked and reached for a cigarette.

The man stared at him curiously, then at the fuselage. His eyes ranged along the side where a dozen punctures showed like staring hollow eyes.

"Are you—all right, sir?"

"Quite, Sergeant." Courtney touched a match to his cigarette. "By the way, when you patch her, I'd like it if you'd just forget to mention——"

"Yes, sir. Very good, sir." His beady eyes twinkled.

Courtney turned on his heel and started for the squadron bar. As he passed the headquarters office Major Brand signaled to him from the door. He approached casually and saluted.

"Courtney, was it you who just brought down a Checkerboard?"

"It was, sir. He was over our lines."

Brand observed him stonily.

"Perhaps you can tell me about an enemy observation balloon that was grounded, too?"

"Why, yes, sir, you see——"

"That was over the enemy lines, of course?"

"It was, Major. I got confused in a cloud bank—strange territory around here for me, sir. When I came out of it I found myself right over him and——"

Brand nodded curtly.

"You win, Courtney. You didn't disobey orders exactly, because you weren't on patrol. Damn it, young man, I congratulate you."

He extended his hand and laughed. Courtney took it.

"Thank you, Major. It was just a bit of luck."

CHAPTER III

COURTNEY was standing alone at the end of the little bar when the morning patrol came home. At first he did not hear the distant drone of the ships. He was deep in his own brooding. When the others quickly set down their glasses and moved to the door he swallowed his brandy and followed them.

He turned his gaze to the eastern horizon. For a long moment he studied the sky, then spoke as though to himself.

"Four coming in."

"Four!" The exclamation sounded like a sob on the voice of Harrington, two weeks out of the cadet class.

They hurried out to the field, wordless and tense. Courtney moved after them leisurely. His face was expressionless. The only emotion that men ever saw there was anger. Even when he laughed it was vaguely without humor, touched too deeply with the cynicism that he wore like a cloak to conceal his secret hurt.

As the planes circled high over the field and shot down, his uncanny vision was proved, for

40

there were four of them. He saw at once that Parker was missing. No leader's pennant fluttered from any of the four. The first plane to flatten off above the ground suddenly dived, struck the hard-packed field with a hollow crash and ground-looped.

Men sprang out to aid. The next ship landed nicely and ran in to the line. The others dropped down in swift succession and their pilots climbed to the ground. Courtney ran out to the overturned ship. He helped to draw Webley-Wentworth from the broken cockpit. The boy tried to stagger to his feet. His head was bloody, but he was smiling.

He drawled an obscene oath as Courtney took his arm.

"What a hell of a mess, Captain." He drew a hand wearily across his eyes. "Here I come home on a crutch and topple over at the last minute."

He rested his weight on the shoulders of two mechanics, and his smile suddenly died.

"Merriwell's down. All shot to hell. And Churchill."

He brightened.

"They got Rex—Parker, y'know. But he landed, damn 'em. Now they'll have to feed him for a while."

"Have you got anything else—except that

one in the head?" demanded Courtney, glancing at the wound.

"That's all. I'm—I'm a bit wobbly, old man. Y'know—" he sagged and was caught in the arms of the men beside him. Courtney strode ahead of them leading the way. Major Brand met them near the hangars. His jaws were set and he was controlling his emotion with an effort.

"Is he badly hit, Captain?"

"Through the head, sir. He trundled the bus home before it got him."

Brand shook his head angrily and bent over the limp figure that was carried up. Young Webley-Wentworth looked very much like a ghastly corpse.

"There's supply truck ready to go." Brand indicated a mud-stained vehicle on the road beyond. "Anybody else?" He stared into the faces of the returned flyers one by one.

"That's all, sir." Bob Buchanan spoke up from his place in the background. "The ships need some patching, though, Major."

Brand nodded and turned to watch the carriers as they bore Wentworth to the truck. Courtney moved inconspicuously beside Buchanan.

"You're a liar," he said in an undertone.

"Get to your quarters. I'll be right along to patch you up."

Ten minutes later he was cutting away Buchanan's boot to reveal a hole that had bored through the calf of his leg.

"If I told the skipper," Buchanan explained, "he'd send me back. And I don't want to miss out on anything, Captain. This won't even cripple me."

Courtney grunted.

"Wait till you try to kick the rudder to-morrow," he said curtly.

"Well," Buchanan shrugged, "what the hell's the difference? The Heinies are so much faster than we that a little delay doesn't change anything."

Courtney washed the wound and bound it. He worked skillfully and without much feeling. Buchanan winced, but made no sound. His face paled, but he hung on to his ghastly smile.

"Did you study for surgery?" he asked presently.

Courtney smiled grimly.

"No. I can kill with less effort than they do."

The boy stretched out in a low chair. The fight was uppermost in his mind. Courtney encouraged him to talk about it, though he knew beforehand the monotonous details.

"We got through one flight of Red-noses. Gad, Captain, you should have seen Wentworth go for them. They ducked out. But he accounted for one of the devils. We wanted to chase them, naturally, but damned if Wentworth would do it. He signaled us back into order and away we went."

Courtney's curt laugh sounded harsh.

"That was your order," he said.

"Quite so." Buchanan observed him doubtfully, uncertain because of his sardonic manner.

"Well," he resumed, "we trundled over to see what we could see, and started home. We hadn't come down ten miles before they were on us. I fancy it was the same flight, because they were red-nosed ships. And they had seven others with 'em this time."

He gazed down at his wrapped leg thoughtfully.

"We didn't have a chance, of course."

Courtney grinned.

"Of course."

"So we gave 'em what ammunition we had and ran."

"Which was perfectly proper and according to instructions."

The youngster stared at him.

"Just what are you driving at, Captain? I don't understand."

Courtney rose and stood looking down at the man.

"You young ass, of course you don't understand." Bitterness made his voice metallic, and his eyes were full of dark fury. "You don't understand that they're sending us up to show off for the infantry. Not to fight. Damn it, Buchanan, we're not being shot in clean combat. We're an outfit of suicides."

The boy was astonished. The thought had not occurred to him before.

"But, Captain, there must be an excellent reason——"

"There is," snarled Courtney. "But they can't expect men to run always. Sometimes, Buchanan, we've got to kill in our own turn."

His rage passed as swiftly as it had come. He smiled and his manner became oddly gentle.

"Forgive me, Buchanan. I forgot myself. I'm not accustomed to formation flying, you see. It's the first time they ever chained me to a group. My nerves seem to be rotten and——"

"Good God, Courtney." Buchanan, in his boyish outburst of sincerity, forgot rank and title and all else save that he was in the presence of a man who had roved alone through the enemy sky. He reached out impulsively and his strong young hand fell upon Courtney's knee.

"I do understand," he said. "We all do." He hesitated, a little embarrassed. "Damn G.H.Q. They'd put an eagle in a cage and expect it to live on canary seed."

The older man continued to smile, and with it there came an amazing change to his seamed young face. It was for a moment as though a mask were drawn aside to reveal the real man. His eyes were full of warmth, and even his voice altered. There was genuine humor in his tone when he spoke. With it was a sincere humility.

"No," he drawled. "The trouble is with me, Buchanan. I've had a lot of luck. I've been pampered and allowed to make my own chart. Now I'm with an outfit that obeys orders and I'm squawking. I ought to be ashamed of myself and I am."

Buchanan laughed.

"I wish to God I had the same reasons for shame that you have," he said simply.

Courtney sobered instantly.

"You wouldn't if you knew my reasons."

Which was as close as he ever got to admitting anything to anybody. It was strange, too, that he should have let down, even to that small extent, to a mere boy. He rose suddenly.

"I'm leading the flight to-morrow."

Buchanan looked up quickly. The news pleased him.

"I'm going to suggest a few days off for you —till that leg heals."

"But Captain, it——"

"You'll have plenty of opportunity. Take a bit of rest, lad."

He wheeled and quit the room. An orderly met him outside and halted with a smart salute.

"Major Brand wishes to see you, sir."

Courtney nodded and followed him. He found Brand at his desk. Again he was motioned to the straight uncomfortable chair.

"You begin to see what we're jolting up against, Courtney." Brand spoke curtly.

"Yes, sir. Butchery by order of G.H.Q."

"I don't like your attitude, Captain."

Their gaze met. In Brand's cold eyes there was the hard metallic gleam of iron discipline. Courtney's dark haggard eyes were full of smoldering fire that seemed about to flame. In that electric instant when lesser men would have lost control they sat rigidly silent. Courtney remembered sharply that he was a soldier.

"I beg pardon, sir."

The major's eyes softened.

"You're under a hell of a strain, Courtney."

"No more than anyone else, sir."

"You're drinking too much."

The bald statement brought a return of the blazing anger, but again Courtney schooled himself.

"If you prefer it, Major, I'll quit."

Brand smiled fleetingly.

"I'll not ask any man to do what I won't do myself. You carry your liquor, Courtney. If it keeps you in line I don't care a damn if you bathe in it."

He glanced at a paper on the desk before him.

"I sent for you because I want you to have a thorough understanding."

"Yes, sir."

Brand tossed over a sheet of flimsy which bore a typed message.

"There's honor and glory," he snapped.

Courtney read a laconic military account of his adventure with the sausage and the checkerboard plane. Suddenly a queer hurt expression came into his eyes as he reached the final instruction. . . .

"In retaliation the enemy sent over a bombing squadron which attacked this sector, killing 11 men and wounding 28. You will instruct your squadron that a similar occurrence will not be tolerated. All fighting must be in formation on this front."

He slowly handed the sheet back to Brand. He offered no comment. The pain in his eyes gave way to ironic humor. He chuckled savagely.

"We are here for show purposes only—at present." Brand continued to study him intently. "As I have stated, we fly over the lines to give our infantry the illusion that they're protected from enemy planes. But if we keep losing men and planes we won't even be able to do that. Is that clear, Courtney?"

"Entirely, sir."

"Very well. I'll give you flight instructions later."

Courtney saluted and left him. The effect of the interview was peculiar. He resolved immediately to fly in formation. He was too much the soldier to mutiny. But on the other hand, he became more than ever ruthless in his mind.

The outward effect was to give him a surface gayety that made itself felt immediately he entered the crowded bar. His laugh was lighter and the sullen glow in his brooding eyes had vanished to give way to a new gleam of amused recklessness.

"Gad, you look contented, almost," said Eustace, himself a very bland young pilot, too inexperienced to have been sobered.

"I shall be directly." Courtney reached for the brandy bottle which Crandall set before him without waiting for his order.

There was a sudden commotion at the door as a newcomer pushed in. He spoke in an undertone to those nearest, and there was a hushed exclamation.

"What rotten luck!"

Eustace swung around hurriedly and called out: "I say, what's that? What's the row?"

But Courtney knew before the answer came. He had heard it come so many times this way that he sensed the news of death before it was actually spoken.

"Poor old Wentworth passed out—on the way to the base."

Courtney drained his drink and walked out of the room. He gazed up at the sky when he got into the open air and drew a long deep breath, then struck off toward the pines that fringed the airdrome. He wanted desperately to be alone. He wished it could have been possible for him to take off and do his thinking ten thousand feet above this hell.

It was not altogether the death of young Webley-Wentworth that brought a swift return of deep-rooted bitterness. He was too familiar with tragedy to have any sentimental theories about it. Now the fact of death was merely a

cause, and this black mood was the effect. He
followed a little-used path that wound along
the extreme edge of the field and presently
threaded into the pines.

He had forgotten Wentworth. His mind was
concerned with the greater problem of those
who still lived. Not just the few young dare-
devils who made up Camel Squadron 31, or
even the larger number who formed the First
Combat Group, but the thousands who must
carry on. Courtney, like every man who had
seen service through those first years, felt certain that the war would go on for years to
come. England might be beaten—obviously
she was beaten then—but she would not quit.

All that was direct and primitive in Courtney's character rebelled against the tactics of
war. It was better, it seemed to him, to kill
one enemy and die, than to let one escape and
live himself, to carry on a show for ground
morale. He hated camouflage in theory and in
fact. His mind struck out sharply and straight
to a point, and he chose to use his body in the
same fashion.

Accordingly, as he flung through the silent
pines he gradually worked up new anger at the
wisdom of G.H.Q., so reinforced by Major
Brand's orders. For men to fly out each day
as helpless targets for the enemy, merely to

brace up the infantry, was a bit of military strategy that he could not force himself to condone. The train of his thought circled around and brought him back again to Webley-Wentworth and his sacrifice.

Suddenly his gaze was drawn by a figure moving among the trees ahead. He saw that it was a girl and she had marked his approach. She was standing in a shadowy grove where the pine trees were less dense. She was young and beautiful, too, with the charm of a hoyden. She was smiling. Her white teeth gleamed, and as he came near she looked up at him with a deliberate affectation of surprise that she could not have felt.

"Hello," Courtney addressed her casually. "What the deuce are you doing?"

His manner pleased her immediately.

"Nothing, Monsieur, nothing at all." Only she gave the word a delightful sibilant pronunciation, as though it were *nossing'*. She was at once childlike and a woman. Her slim piquant face was almost babyish, but her eyes were full of wisdom and her lips were like a red inviting gateway to trouble.

"Nothing," said Courtney, gazing down at her, "is an ideal occupation. Do you live near us, child?"

Her lips pretended to pout, but her eyes were merry.

"Then you have just come to Allonville," she said. "You are—what they call him—cadet? Have you not heard of Celeste?"

Courtney smiled grimly. He had heard of a goodly number of Celestes all along the front. He presumed that this particular one had not been mentioned in his presence. He had scarcely been here long enough to learn these little intimate details.

"I'm sorry." He bowed in mock humility. "I am very ignorant, Celeste. But you see, my dear, I have been here only a few hours."

"Ah, I understand, Monsieur."

Her attempt at English was exquisite and he was enjoying the sound of it . . . the quaint way she said *onerstan'*.

"Where do you live, Celeste?"

She drew herself up proudly.

"I am from Abbeville, Monsieur. I live now at the Château Avignon."

He controlled his swift surprise. The Château Avignon was where Major Brand was quartered. It was an ancient place of stone and no conveniences that lay some little distance in the forest from the airdrome.

"I am Celeste Lyons," she continued, with

simple dignity. "I am your godmother, Monsieur—godmother to the squadron."

Courtney laughed.

"Of course, Celeste. Now I understand. You light candles for us and wish us luck—and steal our cigarettes."

She shrugged.

"I do not steal the cigarettes, Monsieur Captain. Major Brand gives them to me, whenever I wish."

Courtney bowed again and his sardonic smile was lost to her.

"My apologies, Mademoiselle. I should have known——"

She laughed and her hand fell upon his arm.

"I do not mind. You always laugh at me—all of you. But Major Brand he is ver' serious man."

"Yes," Courtney told her soberly, "the major is very serious. He has a great responsibility, Celeste."

They were walking together now, following the winding path.

"He is a ver' old man, too," Celeste said.

Courtney restrained his amusement.

"You must never say that to him, my dear. He isn't old, y'know."

"I have say it to him many times," she protested.

"Doesn't he scold you?"

She shook her head and the dark clusters of hair fell about her temples.

"The major never scolds me, Monsieur. Celeste is not for scolding."

He studied her in a swift sidewise glance which she failed to catch. Her profile was clear and fine against the shadows of the pines. A shaft of light fell obliquely to give a sort of radiance to her skin. Courtney chuckled.

"What, if I may ask, is Celeste for?"

She turned her head quickly and looked straight up into his cynical eyes.

"For love, Monsieur. What else?"

The simple directness of her answer startled him, accustomed as he was to squadron godmothers everywhere. Strangely, he did not smile and his voice was very grave when he answered her.

"That is a very good purpose in life, Celeste. It is by far much finer than being made for hate."

Her slender shoulders lifted in a gesture that was quaint and peculiarly graceful.

"Oh, Celeste can hate, Monsieur. I do hate the enemy."

Courtney observed her steadily.

"That," he remarked, "is propaganda hate. We all hate the enemy. And ten or fifteen years from now we'll be hobnobbing with them as brothers.''

She stared at him.

"Brothers," she repeated scornfully. "No, no, you are ver' wrong, Monsieur. Hate—he live long, but love? Pouf! She come—she go.''

His laugh was bitterly sharp.

"You are very wise about love, Celeste."

Her lips parted in a flashing smile and her eyes met his daringly.

"I have love many times and ver' much, Monsieur."

"But never very long?"

She shrugged again, not offering an answer. She was more interested in this detached soldier whose impersonal manner toward her was so singularly unlike the others.

"An' you, Monsieur," she pursued. "You know about love, too?"

He smiled, but without mirth.

"A bit, my dear."

"An' what have it teach you?"

Courtney returned her gaze with no expression in his own.

"It made me cautious."

That puzzled her.

"I do not onerstan', Monsieur."

Again his crackling laugh brought an expression of curious uncertainty into her eyes.

"You will," he told her, "when you love considerably more and much less often, Celeste."

She was candidly bewildered. Her head shook slowly and she looked down at the path.

"The more I love the more I learn," she said, presently. "Is it not so, Monsieur Captain?"

There was a plaintive quality in her question and she was serious in her attempt to understand him. Courtney refused to be serious on that particular subject.

"It should be that way," he smiled wryly, "but usually, the more we love, the greater fools we become."

They had emerged from the pines, and ahead of them perhaps an eighth of a mile, lay the château. A shell had fallen at one corner, taking away part of the sloping roof and some of the stone from the side. Where the glass had been blown from windows there was canvas nailed to the frame.

"So that is the home of the fairy princess," he said.

Celeste, however, was not in playful mood. His talk had brought upon her one of her rare moments of seriousness.

"Of all of them," she said quietly, "you are the only one who did not make love to me so soon."

Courtney continued to be grave.

"You think I will, sooner or later, Celeste?"

She turned upon him her peculiarly direct gaze.

"You are a soldier, Monsieur, and I am a woman."

"How old are you, Celeste?"

"Eighteen, Monsieur."

"And when did you become—a woman?"

"When the war came."

She was without self-consciousness, entirely at ease. He understood that she had learned to take life as a matter of course. Children and women learned it, even as soldiers and men, he mused. He found himself strangely in sympathy with this child of destiny, pitying her as he pitied the young boys who flew so merrily out to death each morning, when they feared death so very much.

Celeste suddenly stiffened.

"*Mon dieu,*" she exclaimed softly, "run, Monsieur. Look!"

She indicated the château. Standing on a knoll which swept down to them an erect military figure in khaki was watching.

Courtney laughed.

"Why, it is only Major Brand. He is my commanding officer."

She gazed at him wide-eyed.

"But you don't onerstan' Monsieur; the

major, he is ver' jealous man. He will——''
"Come, come, Celeste, he won't be jealous
of me. He knows me rather well. In fact, he
knows my weakness.''

Major Brand was already moving down to
meet them. He walked briskly and as he neared
them he was striking nervously at his polished
boots with his stick. When he came up to them
Courtney saluted easily and smiled.

"Charming place you have, Major."

Brand glanced at him swiftly, then at Celeste.

"Where have you been?" he demanded. His
face was flushed and he controlled his voice
with an obvious effort.

"Ah, you mus' not be angry with Celeste."
She ran to him and seized the lapels of his
tunic. Brand stepped away, turning a hasty,
somewhat embarrassed glance at Courtney.

"I met this charming young person, Major,
when I was walking through the pines," Courtney explained. "She is most interesting, sir."

"Quite so, Courtney. You're not the first of
the squadron to say it." He turned quickly to
Celeste. "You go home and stay there. Must
I tell you, child, my dear, to keep out of the
forest? Confound it, we're too close to the
front——"

She laughed and, reaching up on her toes,
kissed his cheek. She waved to Courtney and

ran lightly up the hill toward the château.

The men stood for a moment in silence watching her.

Courtney said: "I'm sorry to have caused you any embarrassment, Major. I assure you, sir, my coming here was accidental."

"Nothing at all," Brand assured him. "That little vixen will pester me to death, though."

Courtney smiled.

"There are worse ways to die, sir."

Brand observed him swiftly and slapped at his boot again, but said nothing.

"Well, I'll be shoving back, sir. Sorry to have troubled you."

The major nodded. He was standing rigidly when Courtney left him, lost in thought.

CHAPTER IV

For purposes of convenience the squadron kept a blackboard in the bar where the flights were posted each night in chalk. Constant erasure of names gave it a dirty surface, but the board was singularly appropriate there. Certainly no member of any flight ever missed it.

Major Brand, of course, detailed the flights, and his adjutant, the bland Lieutenant Bathurst, maintained a properly typewritten list of names. But for squadron use the blackboard served perfectly.

Accordingly, when Courtney drifted back into the room his gaze went to the chart automatically. There was the list for A Flight, with his name heading it as commander. Directly below it he read the name Scott. He stared and walked quickly up to scan the others at closer range. Selfridge and Woolsey, of course, he remembered. There were three vacancies.

He turned to find Vardon watching him. Vardon was skipper of B Flight.

"Who the deuce is this Scott?"

Vardon's smile was ironic.

"Why, my dear captain, he is *the* Scott—the Honorable Douglas Scott, y'know, of London."

"Good God! Douglas Scott? He's a child, Vardon."

"You know him, then?"

"Of course I know him. When did he come to this hell-hole?"

"Really, old man," Vardon's tone was amused, "he's not such a boy. I've been having a look at the squadron records. He's twenty, old dear. Four years younger than you, my boy."

Courtney observed him patiently.

"Quite so." His voice fell flat. "But Vardon," he indicated the cluttered room as though it was the whole universe, "he hasn't been aged in this."

Vardon shrugged and reached for his half-empty glass.

"Where is Scott?" Courtney asked.

Vardon finished the drink. He said: "If I'm not mistaken you'll find him looking over our crates. He's still young enough to think they're decent."

Courtney nodded and went out abruptly. He saw Douglas Scott standing motionless beside a Camel. He recognized the slender figure, the clean lines of his young jaw as he gazed upward at the cockpit. He had known the youngster rather well back home. Scott sensed his approach and wheeled. His eyes lighted and he came on with both hands reaching out.

"Dick, it's good to see you. I had no idea you were attached here until——"

"Raw material, Doug, both of us. I'm a stranger, y'know."

Their hands met and clung for an instant while the younger man gazed curiously into Courtney's eyes.

"You've changed, Dick. You're—" he broke off shortly.

Courtney laughed.

"Say it, fellow," he used the familiar phrase of their acquaintance in London and in youth that was young. "I've begun to look like a washout."

Scott dropped a protesting hand on his arm.

"Not that. It's just that you're tired—worn out. It must have been hell. I've tried no end to break through. No luck, though, till this year."

"How many hours solo?"

Scott flushed.

"Twenty-five, Dick."

"Good enough. You're a veteran, Doug. We've had some come up here with less than ten hours."

He hesitated a little awkwardly, then nodded toward the squat farmhouse that was headquarters.

"Have you seen our mess room—and bar?" Scott chuckled.

"First thing, y'know. Let's go, Dick."

Again he caught something furtive in Courtney's eye.

"What's up? Anything wrong, Dick?"

Courtney grunted sourly.

"No, damn it. I was thinking, that's all. I don't do it very often any more."

"Thinking what?"

"I wondered, Doug, if—well," he faltered lamely, "you spotted me so damned quickly. My face, I mean. Y'see, old fellow, I've been hitting it a bit too much. I—I was a little ashamed."

Scott's quick laugh was full of relief.

"Forget it. It's all you've had to cheer you. Good God, as though I'd condemn you."

They were moving back toward the farm. Courtney studied the ground and slowly shook his head.

"I know you wouldn't," he muttered. "It's a guilty conscience, I suppose. I'm damning myself, though."

Suddenly he straightened his head and laughed.

A First National Picture.   THE FAST THINNING RANKS LINE UP FOR RATIONS.

The Dawn Patrol.

"There's a consolation," he added. "I'm not making a funnel of myself because I can't help it. By God, it's because I want to."

Scott gripped his arm in a powerful hand and his clear eyes twinkled.

"That's just a mood, Dick. We'll have a spot or two and cheer us up."

They halted abruptly, listening to the doubtful harmony of a chorus. Courtney recognized Vardon's husky baritone leading:

Take the cylinders out of my kidneys,
Take the scutcheon pins out of my brain,
Take the cam-box from under my backbone,
And assemble the motor aga-a-i-n!

The funereal dirge ended on a wailing note of agonizing discord and Scott laughed.

"Good heavens, Dick, you can't be serious after hearing that. *Allons!*"

They burst into the group and a shout of welcome greeted them.

* * * * * * *

Over at the office Lieutenant Bathurst was pacing the littered floor. He watched the window for a sight of Major Brand. Twice he had told G.H.Q. over the wire that he would find the squadron commander instantly. Brand strode in as the buzzer struck again. He answered it himself, studying meanwhile with his bloodshot eyes a half-empty whisky bottle on his desk. The voice at the other end was rasping.

"Certainly I understand," snapped Brand. "Yes . . . bomb the bridgehead at N-Seventeen."

He growled harshly.

"Hell, it can't be done . . . no. . . . I'm damned if I will . . . won't send men into it. . . ."

He bent his head as a burst of profanity sped from the distant headquarters.

"Not by a damn sight," he barked, after a pause. ". . . Because it's in a nest of anti-aircraft guns . . . in the field just beyond the bridge there's a flight of ten Fokkers——"

Again G.H.Q. interrupted. Brand grinned hollowly.

"Of course." His voice was edged. "That doesn't matter if we destroy the bridge."

Another crackling on the wire. The major shrugged.

"No," he said wearily. "You needn't try elsewhere . . . haven't we taken on every job you suggested? . . . All right . . . we'll bomb your damned bridge"

He hung up and scrawled a hurried note on a pad. He drew the bottle toward him and poured a three-finger drink into a glass.

"Get Courtney."

He swallowed the liquor in a gulp. The telephone shattered the brief silence.

"Well?" His staccato growl was bitter.

"Artillery position V-Ten," came the reply. "Two planes of your squadron just brought down an observation plane here. Want the eyewitness record, sir?"

Brand shook his head.

"You're off. We haven't any ships over your line."

"Number three-o-eight and three eleven, sir."

"What's that?"

The voice at V-Ten repeated the numbers.

Brand spat an angry oath.

"Are they out of it?" he snarled.

"Can't tell, sir. They were drawing heavy fire."

"Thanks."

He looked across the desk at Bathurst.

"Courtney and Scott—probably drunk."

He rose and sat down abruptly. His fingers drummed on the desk.

"It's a funny world, Bathurst . . . when you can hate a man, yet tear yourself to pieces worrying about him."

The adjutant nodded moodily.

"Responsibility, Major. Like a woman yanking a kid out the street—then beating hell out of him.''

Brand studied him. His tone was peculiarly level.

''Courtney hates me just as cordially. Thinks I enjoy this rotten business of sending kids out to die. Now I've got to tell him to take 'em out again.''

He looked up from his desk and his lips curled in a twisted smile.

''He'll stare at me—and I'll know what he's thinking.''

The heavy drone of two planes diving with power on drew their taut nerves to the breaking point. Bathurst sprang to the window.

''They're home, sir.''

''Get Courtney in here. Have seven ships ready in thirty minutes.''

''Very well, sir.''

Bathurst ran out to the field. Two planes flattened off and roared down to three-point landings. He gave hurried instructions to the field sergeant and trotted to the line. Courtney was already on the ground removing his helmet. Scott was grinning over the side at him.

''Cheerio, Dick.''

''Like it?''

''First rate.''

Scott climbed down and Courtney, observing

his plane, suddenly found a ragged tear in the fabric just behind the seat.

"Hello." He indicated the hole.

"Yeah, that burst fairly turned her over."

Courtney spread his palm beside the scar. Five inches forward the bullet would have bored into the pilot.

"Close, fellow."

"Quite, but far enough." Scott was drawing a package of cigarettes from his pocket. He offered it to Courtney, who began to feel for a match. Scott found one. He struck it and held the flame as his companion bent down. Courtney watched his hand. It was steady. He inhaled deeply and met Scott's gaze.

"You'll do."

Bathurst approached them.

"The major wants you, Captain."

Courtney chuckled.

"All right. I'll be along."

But when he moved away with Scott they headed first toward the bar. A truck had drawn up before the headquarters office. Six laughing youngsters sprang out, dragging their luggage after them. They were close enough so that Courtney and Scott could make out the pathetic youth of their faces.

"Replacements." Courtney was suddenly hard and grim again.

His companion shrugged.

"At this rate," he muttered, "the next batch will come up with wet nurses."

Courtney was silent. They drank hurriedly without the usual bantering toast.

"What do you suppose the major wants, Dick?"

"He's going to give me hell."

"For what?"

Courtney gazed at him moodily.

"You'll be getting it, too. We're not supposed to go out skylarking, y'know. Damn it, I didn't intend to do it."

Scott mixed water with his whisky. It gagged him a little even then. Courtney drank his neat and pretended to not observe his companion's discomfiture. He set the glass down.

"I'd suggest another," Scott said.

"A bit later— Cheerio."

He went unhurriedly to the office. Bathurst pointed to the door and smiled. He walked in casually. Brand was seated at his desk. He was obviously in a black mood.

"So you're back?"

Courtney sat carelessly on the edge of the desk and helped himself to a cigarette.

"The Fokker attacked us," he said evenly.

Brand sprang from his place. His face was flushed and his voice trembled.

"Courtney, you've been raising merry hell even in the few hours you've been here. This is once too often. I've stood for it because I've counted on you—to help these kids—pull them through. Their lives depend on you."

He paused. His eyes were flaming.

"But you don't care a damn. If that Heinie had set you down, whom could I depend on to get the patrol through?"

He talked with controlled bitterness. It was more venomous than any involuntary burst of anger.

Courtney studied him gravely. There was the discreet understanding between them now that rank was forgotten. This was a thing for men to settle, each in his own fashion.

"That's the way you look at it, Brand." Courtney's voice was steady. "You refuse to understand. I'm not a butcher either, but I'm the one who has to lead these kids. They can't fly. They haven't had the training. Yet it's my job to put them into canvas coffins. I'll fly alone, Brand. Then I'll be responsible for no one except myself."

"I'm responsible for you, Courtney," the major snapped. "And I'm going to shoulder that responsibility, do y'understand? The whole damned army has been on my neck to strafe a bridge——"

Courtney stiffened and leaned forward.

"You mean——"

Brand's finger touched a map he held up.

"That's the place—N-Seventeen. I've ordered your ships on the line. You've got about thirty minutes to get going."

Their gaze met harshly.

"Number Two flight isn't back yet. I'm short three men," Courtney said.

"Take three of the replacements."

"Those boys who just came in?"

Brand sprang to his feet. His face became livid and his blazing eyes had the sudden gleam of insanity. He cursed vilely.

"Don't stare at me, damn you. Get out—bomb that bridge."

Courtney rose, buttoning his leather tunic. He was suddenly cool, smiling.

"Right-o."

He turned unhurriedly and went out. But once in the open he fell into a dog trot toward the mess room. When he pushed into the bar he found Scott instantly. His gesture was almost imperceptible. Scott joined him.

"What's up, Dick?"

Courtney told him. The curt announcement brought a reckless laugh to Scott's lips. He was eager to be off. Then he caught the expression in Courtney's eyes. His smile died.

"What's the jam, fellow?"

Courtney's dark eyes were roving over the faces of the newcomers beyond them, six boys who believed that war was a great adventure.

"We have to take three of them, Doug."

He set his jaws grimly and strode toward them. They faced him.

"I'm Courtney—skipper of A Flight," he announced.

They stiffened and their hands rose abruptly to salute. The foremost among them, a blond youth of perhaps eighteen, drew a sheet of official paper from his blouse.

"Hollister, second lieutenant, sir—reporting for duty from pilot pool."

Courtney glanced at the paper. The others stood before him still at attention. He smiled coldly.

"Break off—you're out of school now."

They relaxed, still a little uncertain. Courtney's smile grew warm and his hard eyes softened. The boys were more at ease.

"That's better. You make me feel more comfortable."

His voice had become jovial. Something inside him seemed to melt as he watched their young faces, eager and clear-eyed. He fought down his impulsive pity and his voice crackled again.

"How many hours for each of you?"

"Fourteen, sir," said Hollister.

The others snapped their meager solo records in the brisk manner of a roll call.

"Nine."

"Sixteen."

"Thirteen."

"Twenty-one."

"Seven—and a half, sir."

Courtney gazed at the last.

"And a half," he repeated. His curt laugh sounded brutal. "Thanks."

He chose the three men with the highest records.

"All right, Hollister—Blane—and you, Machen. Get out on the line."

They flung out of the room elated. Their companions stood crestfallen. Courtney strode to the blackboard. He scrawled hurriedly in the blanks of his own flight, adding the new names. When he faced the group again his eyes were flaming with the rage that worked in his mind. His glance went swiftly to Scott and leaped to Crandall behind the bar. Before he spoke Crandall had set a bottle on the worn counter, beside it a glass.

Beside him Scott ranged with Selfridge and Woolsey, who were going over. They were discussing the detail casually, without excitement or anticipation. Courtney drank in silence. At the sudden burst of deep-throated engines on the field he nodded curtly and started out.

Brand awaited them. The trio of youngsters was standing before him struggling to keep the awe from their faces. Mechanics suddenly switched off and there was abrupt silence. The major nodded to Courtney.

"Everything all right?" he demanded curtly.

"Quite all right."

Brand studied him keenly.

"You'll have to go in low—and fast, Courtney. You'll get one chance at the bridge, perhaps, before the Fokkers get up."

Courtney merely nodded. Brand observed the new pilots mechanically. His words were equally mechanical.

"If anybody is forced down, set fire to your ship. Give no information except your name and squadron. Is that clear?"

The swift expressions of realization that flashed on the faces of the slim youngsters before him were controlled instantly, but not so soon that they escaped the expectant eyes of the older men. Selfridge grinned.

"The crates usually burn before they hit bottom," he suggested lightly.

Woolsey alone laughed as Brand nodded curt dismissal.

"All right." His voice was crisply impatient. "Hit the gun and—good luck."

He looked directly into Courtney's eyes when he said that last. But Courtney was giving laconic instructions to the youngsters.

"Hollister, take second position left. You're third, Blane."

They smiled their appreciation. He had marked their companionship and meant that they should fly together. He spoke curtly to Selfridge. With a covert glance at the new men he gave an unspoken order; the veteran understood. He was to watch over them in flight.

They climbed swiftly to their places. The engines stuttered for an instant, then sounded their thunderous chorus. The slip streams sent up whirling clouds of dirt and bits of paper. Men were grinning from cockpit to cockpit as they adjusted helmets and toyed with the throttles. Courtney gave his motor one last vicious stream of fuel and abruptly waved.

His ship ran out into the wind with its leader pennant streaming. He pulled up into a steep climb. As the shock of ground-running ceased he stared back and down. Scott was roaring after him and in precise order the others. He held the stick back until they were all clear of the ground, then flattened off. He watched until they fell into formation. When the flying

V was perfected he waved once again and opened the throttle wide.

Down on the field Major Brand and Bathurst stood watching until the flight became a tiny wedge in the distant sky. A woefully futile wedge, the major was thinking, with which to pry an entry into the German empire. He wheeled abruptly and moved toward the office. Bathurst trudged after him in silence.

Brand paused in front of his untidy desk. He suddenly picked up the empty whisky bottle that was standing there and flung it into a corner. It crashed against the wall and burst. Without pausing to observe the wreckage he went to a cupboard, where he found a fresh bottle. He carried this back to the desk, sat down and began to remove the tissue wrapping with methodical care.

Bathurst had stared briefly at the broken bottle, then turned again to the window, where he continued to watch the sky.

"Seven—instead of four hundred," he droned dismally. "Theirs not to reason why," he commenced to quote.

Brand jerked at the wrapping. His voice broke in a quivering sob of futile anger. His nerves were near the point of collapse.

"Damn you, Bathurst—shut up—get to hell out of here."

The adjutant glanced at him and shrugged. "I'm sorry."

He left the little room unobtrusively. Brand drew the cork from the bottle and poured a deep drink. His hand shook when he raised the glass. He swallowed it hurriedly and poured another. A slow flush spread on his cheeks, as though a gray corpse had suddenly responded to the inexorable call of life. His eyes found the round bland face of an alarm clock on a shelf. Its steady ticking was the only sound in the room.

Like a man who is hypnotized by some intangible power that sways him despite every struggle of his will, he kept staring at the clock. He did not remove his gaze from it even when he poured more whisky, nor did he look away when he tilted the glass to let the burning liquor slip down his parched throat.

He watched the minute hand. Each time it paused fleetingly over a little black line he reminded himself that Courtney and his flight were nearer their objective. Subconsciously he was counting the monotonous ticking of the cheap works.

It was not until the liquor gurgled thinly when he poured that Brand took his eyes from the clock. It was to see then that the bottle was more than three quarters empty.

CHAPTER V

COURTNEY'S familiarity with the Rolands of
the enemy caused him to climb well above the
clouds almost immediately. The chart that was
strapped on his knee showed a red-penciled
circle where the bridgehead should be. For the
rest he depended on his instruments and instinct.

The flight swung up behind him in the manner of a flock of wild ducks with confidence in
their gander. The enemy line curved down
from Spincourt to Etain and he kept watching
the sun-bathed sky above them and the cloud
banks below for any fleeting interruption of
the monotony. When the instrument panel indicated that they were some thirty-two kilometers west of Etain, Courtney tripped the
trigger of the Vickers gun that was adjusted
directly in front of him, in a test.

He flung one hand up in signal to the others
and each in turn they blazed into the air. They
were flying Bristol fighters, each ship with an
improvised bomb rack. Like his own, they had,
too, the Vickers guns, and above and in front of

each pilot the usual Lewis gun for emergency.
Courtney next lowered the Lewis and sent a
second hail of steel into space. The flight followed his example and he signaled back that all
was well.

At a point which he judged to be somewhere
over Etain, when the altimeter needle was quivering on the numeral 14, Courtney shoved the
stick gently forward and kicked the rudder for
a sweeping bank into the south. He glanced
over his shoulder at the flight and bobbed his
head in answer to Scott's cheerful wave.

By every calculation he judged that they
would nose out through the clouds within two
minutes to find their objective clearly visible.
He wiggled the ailerons, and with a sweeping
glance over the side shot down in a power dive.
Almost immediately he discovered that his calculations had been wrong by ninety seconds.
The Bristol bored into the open, and as he eased
the dive to a long oblique, Courtney saw the
bridgehead.

It lay about a mile to the west. Instantly he
dived again with the flight on his tail. When
he flattened off at a thousand feet he quit the
controls entirely to stand up in the cockpit.
He spread his arms in a gesture that Scott and
the others grasped without hesitation. They
promptly widened the formation.

Just before he roared over the bridge Courtney released his bomb. He understood that it
would fall in a curve at a muzzle velocity of a
hundred miles an hour. As he pulled back the
stick to climb, the anti-aircraft guns began to
speak, and down in the field beyond a Fokker
already was running across the ground into the
wind.

He laughed as he saw the black cloud spurt
upward from the bomb. It was no direct hit,
but the roadway was blocked. Behind him
Selfridge had better luck. He planted one of
the little black eggs squarely on the bridge.
Scott, as Courtney anticipated, released his
charge too late, forgetting in his excitement
that a bomb must start before the plane is
fairly over its target.

In swift succession the others dropped their
grim supercargoes and followed him up.
Courtney was heading for a cloud bank that
offered some chance of escape from the speedy
Fokkers. He waved, and when he stared back
over the tail he was laughing aloud, unaware
of it in the savage strain of his emotion.

The bridgehead was wrecked. Moreover, the
road on either side of it would offer sorry passage for motor lorries and troops for many a
day. His last glimpse of the scene showed him
a smoking mass of confusion, but with it

came a distinct view of the climbing Fokkers.

The real hell was yet to come. For a moment, as the Bristol vanished into the wet vastness of the clouds, Courtney chuckled to himself. In the next instant he recalled the boy Hollister, and his companions, Blane and Machen. His laughter died on a note of guttural anger. He roared into sunlight and kept the nose up. He half-turned and saw the others as they flashed from the mist, each ship glistening.

At eight thousand feet he leveled off and headed west. He kept staring back and down at the clouds. The Fokkers should be coming through. As he faced ahead his eyes widened beneath his goggles and an exclamation escaped him involuntarily. The Fokkers had outdistanced them below the clouds and were climbing up to block their flight ahead. He saw them rising from the mist like gleaming black wasps. Their noses were carmine, as though they had been dipped into blood.

"Swine."

The hot blood raced through his veins protesting against the trick. With the advantage their own in any event, they had resorted to that! He turned his head and for a fleeting instant observed the flight. Gloved hands rose above the cockpits in signal and he knew that they were prepared.

Air strategy, Courtney told himself, required that he should run. He counted nine Fokkers. They were between A Flight and home and they had the advantage of greater speed and ample fuel, to say nothing of adequate ships and ammunition. Courtney grinned and it distorted his face.

He might fly back into German territory, or dive to destruction over the enemy lines eight thousand feet below. Or, as another alternative, he could climb with his flight until the Fokkers sped up over them to pick off each ship in turn.

He chose the only course that appealed to him. His Bristol nosed up sharply toward the Fokkers. In graceful formation the others followed him. A red-nosed plane suddenly poised on its tail, keeled over in a roll and swept straight down over him, firing as it came.

Courtney promptly stalled. He felt the ailerons lose their lifting power as they dragged. The Bristol mushed through the air crazily, with her nose above the path of flight, so that the Fokker's fire went wild. In that instant Courtney shoved the stick, and as he gained flying speed, opened the throttle. He looped up, tripping the Lewis gun in a direct fire on the dodging black plane.

All about him now the air was blazing. His eyes swept the scene for a glimpse of familiar ships, but in that confused mingling he could make out only a fantastic panorama of sky and clouds with maddened insects indistinguishably tangled. He came up beside the Fokker that had attacked him. The wing tips almost brushed. He stared across at the pilot who was tugging at his controls.

"Jammed, damn you!"

He left his own controls and half rose as he drew his automatic. This was something he was familiar with. Here was the way they fought during the first year, wing to wing, with rifles and revolvers. Courtney grinned cruelly as he brought the heavy weapon down. He pressed evenly on the trigger. The pilot opposite him suddenly stiffened. Their gaze met for an instant. Then the Fokker began to nose down. As it turned over beneath him Courtney saw the pilot plunge out.

Courtney dropped back into his seat in time to kick the rudder for a bank as a second ship bored down over him. In the maneuver he saw two Fokkers riding over a Bristol. He recognized Blane in the doomed and blazing plane that was already going down. Another Bristol was spinning over the German. As it straightened out of the maneuver Courtney laughed again. He recognized the gallant Scott, already pouring steel into the red-nosed killer.

Courtney fought mechanically. It was his way. Even when he saw young Machen fall back into his control seat with his arms flung out in a final gesture of resignation, he manipulated the controls of his own ship methodically and as methodically pressed the trigger of his Lewis gun. It was a process of elimination. Somebody's turn was next.

He thought subconsciously while he looped and dived among the planes. He even tried to count the Bristols. He succeeded presently. There were four of them still. A third Fokker loomed just over his nose. Courtney pulled back the stick and went at him. The startled pilot rolled over to escape a head on. In the split second of his bewilderment Courtney dived with his gun spitting. The Fokker burst into red and yellow flame.

"Burn, damn you—in hell!"

He was a lunatic with a fascination for killing. Whatever there had been of humanness in his soul had become shriveled now, so that it did not function. He gave no conscious thought to himself. Whatever he did to save himself was mechanical. His feet and hands reached for controls and trigger with the monotonous regularity of pistons that work in an oiled groove. His face was a ferocious mask.

The thing that brought him out of the subconscious and into himself was a whirling glimpse of the earth.

It puzzled him. For a fragment of time he was alone. He saw no other planes. He heard only the bitter irregularity of his motor. He fondled the throttle and hit the fuel pump instinctively. The engine burst into harmony. He centered the controls and the Bristol flew suddenly on an even keel.

Courtney knew then for the first time that he had fought down through the clouds. He pulled the stick to climb back to the flight. From the clouds just above him there came a Bristol and behind it another. Two others flashed out far ahead in the west and half a mile on his left he saw a black streak plunging earthward, leaving a comet's tail that reached up into the banks.

From force of habit he glanced at his watch. The whole beastly affair had commenced seven minutes earlier.

Courtney wiggled his ailerons and headed for home. Three ships fell in behind him. He found himself wondering about the third washout. He hoped vaguely that Scott had come through. At that moment there sped from the cloud bank a fourth plane and he saw that it was a Bristol. It plunged straight over him and zoomed, stood for an instant on its tail, then fell back in a spin and at the exact level of the flight, straightened off. Courtney grinned. He recognized Scott at the controls.

They ventured low as they flung across the lines. A futile Archie sent up lazy puffballs loaded with vicious shrapnel that fell short. Over the British front Courtney shot down to roar above the shattered trees with scant margin. The infantrymen waved at them from the trenches and made strange gestures. Courtney smiled moodily. It was difficult, he thought, to convince an infantryman that a flyer had anything but a soft berth.

Allonville Forest spread beneath them presently, and, like a bald spot on a huge dark head, the airdrome. He dived steeply. As he set the Bristol down and taxied to the line, Courtney stripped off his helmet. He switched off, and before the prop quit spinning he was on the ground. Scott's ship rolled in beside his own. For an instant Courtney's reddened eyes were full of anxiety. Then Scott sprang down.

"All right, fellow?" Courtney spoke in an undertone.

"Yes."

The other planes were on the line. The last one in taxied erratically and the pilot slumped in his seat. Courtney ran toward him. It was Hollister.

"Are you hit, old man?"

Hollister forced himself upright and Courtney half lifted him to the ground. The boy was stricken by a terrible retching. When he could speak, he raised his head. Terror still lurked in his eyes.

"Bob—went down." His voice broke in a sob.

Courtney's face hardened. He understood the effect of shock.

"Snap out of it, Hollister."

"And—Machen," the boy cried.

Courtney and Scott caught him as he sagged.

"Better have a spot," said Courtney. "It'll help your guts."

They led him toward the farm.

"I don't—want a drink," he protested. "I —just want to be alone."

Courtney nodded silently to Scott as they passed the door of the mess room.

"Go ahead. I'll be along directly."

He led Hollister into the bunk room. The boy sank down upon a cot beside a litter of stuff from his army trunk that was open on the floor.

Beside it was another, still locked. Hollister stared at it.

"Bob didn't—have time to—unpack," he muttered.

Courtney bent over him.

"Steady, Hollister. Play the game, old man. You can't let yourself go."

The youngster gazed up at him, intrigued by the strange softness of his voice. He smiled faintly as he saw the warmth in Courtney's eyes. He nodded abruptly as he began to understand.

"I know, Captain. You've got the thing down. No emotion—no let-down. We can't fight and—be human too."

Courtney smiled grimly.

"You're lucky, Hollister, to learn that so soon."

His bronzed hand, stained with oil and calloused from contact with the controls, fell lightly for a moment on the boy's shoulder. A wordless understanding was with them in that instant. Courtney turned and left him alone.

He went unhurriedly to Brand's office. His face was expressionless when he paused, framed in the door. Brand was standing at his desk a little unsteadily. The bottle before him was quite empty. The alarm clock was ticking, but that was the only sound.

"We scored direct hits on the bridge—wiped it out." Courtney's voice was peculiarly without feeling.

"Yes."

"Two men lost—Blane and Machen."

"Yes, I know. That's all, Courtney."

When Courtney's flat leather back turned on him Brand sank into his chair. He waited until Courtney had gone, then picked up the telephone. In a flat, toneless voice he identified himself.

"You can report N-Seventeen wiped out."

The voice at G.H.Q. crackled back to him. Brand twisted in sudden torture. He fairly bellowed into the transmitter.

"Yes, by God, wiped out, I said. Is that enough?"

Headquarters spoke again. This time it was a question.

"Two," he snarled. "Both replacements just up."

He jerked the receiver from his ear at the next sentence. The rasping voice sounded distinctly:

"That's good work, Brand—only two this time."

Slowly he placed the instrument back on his desk. All the rage vanished from his face and a queer hurt expression took its place. He

stared at the telephone and repeated in a dull
monotone:

"Only two."

He sat motionless for a long time, gazing va-
cantly into space. He was still there an hour
later when the faithful Bathurst came in. He
gazed at his superior curiously.

"Dinner is ready, Major."

"Never mind, Bathurst. I'm not hungry."

"Is there anything——"

"No. Go on. I'm all right."

Bathurst marked his haggard unshaven face,
the feverish eyes, and paused uneasily.

"If you're ill, Major——"

Brand made an impatient gesture with his
hand.

"I'm all right, I tell you. Damn it, Bathurst,
don't baby me."

The adjutant observed him patiently with
eyes that were full of sympathetic understanding. He went out and joined the squadron in
the mess room. He found Buchanan there, with
Woolsey and Selfridge and the rest of them.
Most of the others were strangers, replacements. Buchanan was trying to conceal a slight
limp. Courtney was leaning against the bar
smiling at him.

"I knew damned well that nick would bother
you, Buchanan."

Buchanan chuckled.

"A little."

The talk was all of the dog fights and the action of the day. The young strangers were subdued, trying to appear nonchalant, but not yet able to present expressionless faces to this casual acceptance of death.

At a round table beside the wall Scott and Vardon were drinking from the same bottle. Courtney and Selfridge joined them.

"I say, Dick," Scott motioned to a vacant chair beside him, "something ought to be done about that beastly battery south of Etain. They were placing those hundred-an'-fives right up against us."

Courtney shrugged.

"Well, they got some of their own dirty dose. I saw one Fokker fairly drip right down on 'em."

The boy Hollister half turned at the indifferent voice. His eyes were drawn and pain still contorted his face. He had forced himself to join the others. He could not longer bear the sight of that unlocked trunk in the bunk room. Courtney glanced up to catch his gaze.

Suddenly Vardon leaned back in his chair and raised a tumbler of brandy. He burst into the chorus of a squadron favorite:

So stand by your glasses steady;
  This world is a world of lies.
Here's to the dead already;
  Hurrah for the next man who dies!

Scott was leaning against the wall with his chair tipped back on two legs, his eyes closed. Courtney observed him and smiled.

"Sleep through it if you can," he challenged.

Scott opened his eyes drowsily. He gazed at Vardon.

"Is that spasm done with?" He rose. "Then I'll play 'Poor Butterfly' some more."

The dull needle ground plainly into the disk in prelude. The door crashed open almost as the first rasping notes filtered out. Bathurst came in, followed by Brand. The major jerked his head impatiently and Scott turned off the instrument. Brand glanced around swiftly from one face to the next. He paused when he came to Courtney.

"Sorry to disturb you, gentlemen." He coughed. His voice was almost apologetic, but his smile was bitter. "It seems that we have a bit more work ahead of us."

He drew a sheet of scratch paper from his tunic.

"I've just been advised that we're ordered out again in the morning. There's an advance going up. G.H.Q. wants us to patrol four kilometers behind the enemy lines.''

His eyes wandered uneasily beneath the concentrated stares that turned on him. In them there was mingled amusement, an element of surprise, and with it the swift anticipation of an end to this brief boredom.

He glanced at the paper in his hand.

''Strafe any reinforcements and munition convoys, of course. When the barrage commences, B Flight will cover our observation ships. Cleaver and Burt—you're detailed to A Flight. Greer, you're with B.''

As he spoke the names he turned his tired bloodshot eyes on the men.

''Nice quiet little jaunt.'' That was from Murell, a replacement trying to be nonchalant.

Brand stared at him and said nothing. There was a silence.

''You will take off at four,'' he said directly. ''I will have detailed instructions for each flight.''

He wheeled and went to the bar. His hand shook when he lifted a glass so that the liquor spilled. Courtney rose lazily from his place and went to the blackboard. He picked up a dirty rag from the ledge and smeared out the names of Machen and Blane. Behind him young Hollister was staring with something in

his eyes not far removed from madness. He
half raised his hand in a gesture of protest,
then let it fall back.

Courtney scrawled in the names of Cleaver
and Burt. When he quit the board Hollister
was leaving the room, moving at a peculiar stag-
gering gait toward the door. Scott reached
over and released the starting lever of the
gramophone. The grinding music burst forth
anew. Scott grinned sleepily and poured himself a heavy drink.

"Did y'see Hollister, poor kid?" His voice
was thick and he was becomming maudlin.

"What hit him?" Vardon asked.

"He was watching Dick wipe the slate—
couldn't stand it."

Courtney looked at him swiftly, surprised.
His face clouded.

"I didn't think of that. The names had to
be changed."

Suddenly he growled an oath.

"That's it. Kids. They can't bear up in
this sort of thing. Why, damn it, Doug, young
Hollister's no older than your kid brother."

Scott smiled drunkenly.

"Gordon," he said, and shook his head
slowly. "Good lad. I went up to school to see
him last time I was home. God, he was proud,
y'know. Thought I was a hero."

Brand paused as he passed their table. He spoke to Courtney.

"Flight leaders will report to me at three."

Courtney said, "Very well, Major."

Brand looked at Scott, then back to Courtney.

"If you want to protect your lambs you'd better lead them over sober."

He left them abruptly. Courtney stared after him. The taut muscles of his jaws were working convulsively. He half rose and sank back. Suddenly he laughed. He reached out and touched Scott's arm.

"Get to shut-eye, Doug. You heard the major."

"Oh, I say, Dick, you go to the devil."

Courtney continued to gaze at him, still smiling.

"Do you go, or do I carry you?" He spoke quietly, but there was no lightness in his tone.

Scott straightened and stared at him wonderingly.

"Well, I'll be damned."

He rose unsteadily and put his hand on Courtney's shoulder.

"Better come an' tuck me in, ol' dear—sing little Douglas t' sleep, what?"

He idled toward the bar, had another drink as a gesture of good-natured defiance and went out, struggling ridiculously to keep a straight

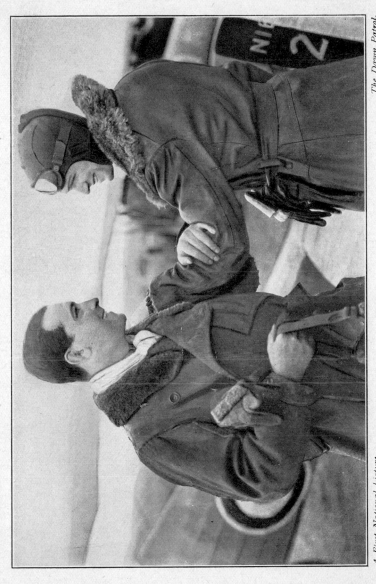

A First National Picture.   *The Dawn Patrol.*

DICK COURTNEY AND HIS PAL DOUGLAS SCOTT DEFY THE SQUADRON COMMANDER'S ORDERS.

path. For a time the others lingered. Vardon
and Courtney sat alone. They understood the
significance of Brand's manner. But they
drank pleasantly and smiled cheerful good
nights as the others, one by one, or in twos and
threes, drifted to their bunks.

"It may be the big push," Vardon said,
thoughtfully.

His brooding companion shrugged.

"There's one thing we can gamble on," Vardon continued, studying his drink. "When
Fritz sees a squadron coming over he'll know
something's up. We'll have every circus on
this front on our tail, Courtney."

"Probably."

Vardon studied him from half-closed eyes.

"You're sincere about it, aren't you? The
rest of us are liars—even to ourselves. You
honestly don't care a damn, do you, Courtney?"

"Not a damn," Courtney told him steadily.

Vardon asked: "If it's any of my business,
old man, why?"

Courtney faced him.

"I don't quite know myself."

Vardon stood up. He was a little embarrassed.

"Well, a nightcap," he suggested. "And an
eye-opener before we go, what?"

Courtney smiled.

"Bottoms up."

They went out together. On the way to his quarters Courtney stopped in to have a look at Scott. He was lying flat on his back with his arms flung out. His broad white chest was uncovered. Courtney drew the blanket over him and adjusted his arms. Scott sighed.

Courtney went on to his quarters. In the subdued glow of the single lamp he again studied the peaceful face of Mary Cambridge in the silver frame. He read the verse again too, and smiled a little wistfully now. His subtle resentment was gone. Something had come into his soul when the last replacements came into his flight for which he had no accounting. He felt strangely subdued and somehow resigned.

It was a humility that was new to him and with it there came an understanding that he had never possessed before. He almost began to understand Brand and he was striving to grasp the problems which caused the army gods to rule as they did.

He sat for a long time studying the face. His mind wandered without direction. . . .

"And the High Soul climbs the High Way
And the Low Soul gropes the Low . . ."

There was something wrong about that philosophy, he told himself. Was it not possible for a high soul to grope, too? Might not a lofty purpose somehow fail? For himself, in his cold introspection, he held no brief. He did not pretend that his soul was one of the so-called high ones. But this one thing he knew. Whatever he had done, whatever he might do, he had never intentionally resorted to a mean thing. . . .

He suddenly flung back his head and laughed. It was a grim sound in the silence there. . . .

"And every man decideth the Way his soul shall go."

He said that aloud and laughed again.

"Like hell he does," he muttered. "Like hell he does."

CHAPTER VI

IN THE drab light that was on the field when the squadron assembled for instructions, the studied nonchalance of the replacements vanished. They were candidly uneasy. Courtney was deliberately brutal. He knew that any show of feeling might play upon a taut set of nerves to snap them. He felt secretly that they would be overwhelmed in the first half-hour of fighting.

The deep-rooted sense of fatalism that he had himself planted and nursed in his own mind, served him well. He was able to curse heartily when he discovered that a dog-pin had worked free from his Lewis gun. It helped him to shrug at the grave voice of Major Brand telling off each flight. He was able, with the false armor of his fatalism, to ward off even a subconscious fear of death.

As he inspected the Bristols of A Flight, and turned a critical gaze on the larger two-place bombers which were to be protected, he smiled curiously. If all of them went down in flames, he told himself, the loss of life would be less than that from a single well-placed shell in a front-line trench. He did not take into consideration the difference between a swift death on the ground and perhaps a brief lingering consciousness aloft.

All about him there was the familiar chaffing under delay. At length Brand gave the signal and each man climbed to his place. Courtney paid attention to his instruments, ignoring the laughing calls that flew from plane to plane along the line. He sat almost indolently in the control seat until the Handley-Page bombers were off. Without a gesture to the men on the ground he sped into the wind after them. The Bristols ran out in order behind him and went up lightly, like swallows in the wake of lumbering geese.

When the last ship vanished in the blue-gray void of the morning sky, Brand still waited on the tarmac. Bathurst, the faithful, stood beside him. The mechanics listened for a time to the dwindling drone of the motors and disappeared. It was yet too early for full dawn, but the eastern horizon was intermittently crimson. The muffled rumble from the front was like thunder in the distance and the glow was suggestive of heat lightning in the summer.

Brand turned on his heel so abruptly that he was a dozen feet on his way back to the office before Bathurst fairly started. The adjutant trudged after him, studying the ground. As he entered the darkened room with its rank smell of liquor and stale tobacco smoke, Brand switched on the light. His gaze went to the clock and traveled to the bottle on his desk. He threw off his jacket and flung himself into the chair.

"All right, Bathurst. There's nothing now."

"No breakfast, Major?"

"No."

The adjutant stood doubtfully. Brand gazed up at him.

"Did you see the way Courtney looked at me?"

"I can't say that I noticed it, sir."

"Umph, you wouldn't."

Brand poured a drink. He emptied the glass at a gulp.

"He gets an expression in his eyes," he resumed thoughtfully, "that a man would have when he looked at a venomous snake."

Bathurst waved a protesting hand.

"Major, your nerves are bad. You imagine——"

"Imagine hell," Brand snarled. "You can't imagine the look in a man's eye, damn it."

Bathurst observed him steadily. When he spoke his voice was full of a quiet strength.

"It seems to me you and Courtney simply misunderstand one another, Major. You're both shooting at the same target, y'know. As a matter of fact, I think the same thing ails both of you."

Brand smiled coldly, but his eyes were curious. Bathurst took his manner as an invitation to go on.

"You hate to send these boys out. So does Courtney. But you're more accustomed to it, being in a position of authority. He's used to cutting off alone. Naturally, he resents discipline. If he didn't, Major, he couldn't be the man he is."

Brand studied the bottle, but he was looking through and beyond it.

He said: "Perhaps you're right, Bathurst. But damn it, he scratches me the wrong way."

Suddenly he straightened. His lined face softened fleetingly.

"But God, how I'd hate to lose him," he added.

Bathurst nodded.

"He has that quality of working on your nerves. He's like—a seventy-seven coming across, sir. Makes one jumpy and unhappy. But he's pretty torn by his own troubles, if I'm any judge."

Brand glanced up quickly.

"What is it that's working on him, Bathurst?
I've heard stories——"

The adjutant shrugged.

"No one knows, Major. I've heard there was
a woman—there usually is, y'know, when a fellow of his sort goes in for the drink—a woman,
or something——"

"I heard the woman story myself."

"Courtney never mentions his past."

Brand was reminded of Celeste Lyons and
her single meeting with Courtney. He
frowned.

"He's the sort who'd play hell with a
woman," he mused, half to himself.

Bathurst observed wisely: "Perhaps. But
on the contrary, it's my opinion he's the sort
with whom a woman would play hell."

"Meaning just what, Bathurst?"

"I think, sir, that Courtney takes love seriously."

Brand laughed.

"Of course, you damned fool. That's the
type that women fall for. The Sir Galahads out
for the Holy Grail."

Bathurst smiled.

"In that case," he conceded, "it should work
both ways for him. I'm not familiar enough
with the opposite sex to be a judge, though."

Brand winced, though the adjutant was inno-

cent enough. When he went out presently,
Brand tried to drive out thoughts of the flight
by thinking of Celeste. He recalled her curiosity about Courtney with a twinge of jealousy.
He knew that in a fair tilt, with Celeste as the
prize, he would be no match for Courtney. Her
manner had made that clear enough.

The thought angered him anew. His mind
kept telling him that he was being unjust, but
his emotions goaded his rage. He had, of late,
become a slave to his emotions anyway, so that
an attempt to reason out a thing of so personal
a nature as this was impossible. He could remember only the peculiar expression in Celeste's eyes when she had spoken of Courtney.

''He is so sad an' so young.''

As though she longed to comfort him.

He stirred uneasily. Celeste was the only
thing left for Brand that was even faintly rem-
iniscent of youth. Frankly, he did not love her.
Neither did he delude himself in the belief that
she loved him. But she gave him comfort and
as much of herself as he required. It was
good to sit opposite her at the table in the
château and listen to her voice, even though he
scarcely heard what she said. He enjoyed her
singing.

He smiled softly. Celeste was exquisite. She
had a way of running her fingers through his

hair that soothed him. Her voice, when she laughed, was silvery. It was golden when she sang. And in the night, when she whispered to him, it was like the voice of a gentle breeze among the pines, crooning and restful. . . .

Her lips were very warm . . . he closed his eyes and visioned white rounded arms . . .

He jerked to attention at the far hum of an approaching plane. He stared at the clock.

"Good God, they're back."

It scarcely seemed possible that he had been lost there in his thoughts for more than an hour and a half. Yet the fiendish clock met his gaze with its bland round face speaking the truth. He thought swiftly that in all existence nothing appears so completely unemotional as a clock.

He sprang to the door and went out. The sky was lighting rapidly. Against the full glow in the east he counted four Bristols. Lumbering after them were the bombers. He breathed heavily as he counted them, four black birds in the wake of as many black wasps. He groaned involuntarily. Then he saw two more of the larger planes coming on at a distance.

He stumbled as he ran out toward the field. Men were pouring from the hangars and the farm. The first Bristol shot down to a reckless fish-tail landing. Brand's military instinct revolted and he determined to speak to the pilot about the care of ships. Then he saw Hollister leap from the cockpit and brace himself against the fuselage as though he had been hurt.

The next ship came down perfectly on three points and glided exactly to the line. Courtney climbed over lazily and pushed his goggles back. The others pointed down in swift succession, and before the last one halted, the land force was surging about them. Hollister stared wide-eyed at the men who surrounded him. He was dazed.

"He's dead."

His voice was unnatural, quavering thinly.

"Scott," he added. "Trying to help me—they got him."

He sagged against his ship. Courtney pushed through the group and halted in front of him. He stared down into the boy's frightened eyes.

"Scott," Hollister said again. "He was—trying to help me."

"Yes?" Courtney's tone was brittle. "What of it? Quit your damned blubbering. You're safe, aren't you?"

The boy gazed at him in stunned horror. He lowered his head and a slow flush crept up from beneath his collar. He turned away and started toward the farm. Selfridge moved toward him impulsively. Courtney motioned to him.

"I wouldn't. Let him have it out alone. He'll come through."

He turned to face Brand. The major eyed him questioningly.

"We broke up the counter-attack—until the Fokkers found us."

"Yes?"

"We lost Woolsey—Cleaver—and Scott."

Brand's eyes grew dull. His jaw moved, but he did not speak. He only nodded. Courtney turned away abruptly. When he reached the bar Murell and Blythe, with some others, were there in advance of him, already seriously engaged in the business of drinking. They fell into sudden silence as he joined them.

"Hello." He went to his accustomed place at the end of the bar. Crandall already had the bottle up.

Mechanically Blythe reached out and touched the starting lever of the gramophone. The disk whirled in its monotonous prelude to Scott's "Poor Butterfly." Courtney lowered his head at the first note. Murell signaled and Blythe switched off, suddenly aware. Courtney gazed at them and his lips curved in a faint smile.

"Go ahead—play it. What does it matter?"

He raised his glass, full to the brim, and drained it. Instantly he refilled it. His hand

was steady. But no one played the gramophone. They talked in subdued tones. Occasionally a glance was turned on Courtney and
swiftly withdrawn. They were embarrassed by
they knew not what. The subject of death
among them was not one to create this unreal
atmosphere of hesitancy. Nor could it be attributed to any outward grief that Courtney
showed.

The strain was relieved by the entrance of
Brand. He wore a peculiar expression of concern and there was outright friendliness in his
voice when he ranged beside Courtney.

"I'm sorry, old man. Is there anything I
can do?"

Courtney's laugh was like a curse.

"Yes—have a drink."

Brand smiled with grim understanding.

"Thanks. I will."

Crandall set a glass before him. Courtney
pushed the bottle closer. Brand poured a drink
in silence, then stood fingering the glass.

"What happened?" His voice sounded impersonal.

Courtney studied the reflection of the light in
his liquor. It glowed amber and seemed to re-
peat itself in his dark eyes.

"After the first barrage," he said quietly, as

though he were launching an account of an ordinary engagement, "we worked over beneath a handy cloud bank—strafing a convoy."

He sipped the whisky.

"Thirteen Fokkers dropped on us from the bank. . . . Woolsey got it before we could fire a shot. . . . Scott and I managed to knock off one apiece. . . . I didn't see Cleaver go . . . don't know what happened to him at all."

He emptied the glass and refilled it.

"Hollister . . . poor devil, funked . . . got in under a Heinie. . . . Scott went to him and . . . two of 'em got over him at once . . . cross-fired him . . . he went down out of control . . . I know that . . . he was in my line of vision . . . he waved . . . and went into a spin."

His voice was listless, droning the account mechanically.

"I went after the first Fokker . . . he dropped back of our lines. . . . I was too busy too see where Scott fell."

He held the glass up before the light beneath his critical gaze and emptied it. Brand finished his drink and set down the empty glass. The door behind them opened and Hollister came in. He went immediately to a chair in a corner and sat down alone. He did not call for a drink, or speak to anyone. His face was gray and his eyes were wild.

"He's going to break," Brand said in an undertone.

"It wouldn't be military. G.H.Q. would protest," said Courtney.

The door smashed in again violently this time. Bathurst paused on the threshold, searched until he found Brand and strode hurriedly to the bar.

"Major, an artillery car is here with a German pilot. They say A Flight brought him down."

"Bring him in," said Brand.

Bathurst disappeared and returned in a few moments accompanied by the German. He was a blond youth with china-blue eyes and an expression of bland innocence.

"Major, Oberleutnant Hartmann," Bathurst introduced them formally, with an amused, gentle bow.

The German stiffened and his salute snapped up from the hip. Brand nodded curtly. Courtney gazed at the prisoner and recognized the face from the fleeting glimpse he had had of it in that careening instant in the air. He smiled.

"Have a drink."

"Thank you, Captain." In decent English.

Courtney himself poured and handed the glass to Hartmann. The German smiled.

"Schnapps," he muttered and licked his lips.

He raised the glass in a gallant gesture. Courtney touched it with his own and they drank. Behind them, Hollister stared with growing disbelief that such things could be. His horror was written on his strained face and his hands kept clenching on the table in front of him. He was struggling to control himself. It was his first experience with a prisoner of war.

Presently he got up and moved uncertainly toward the door. Vardon half rose, then fell back into his place.

"What the hell?" he asked plaintively. "The kid will have to fight it out for himself. There's nothing you can say to him."

Later the prisoner was taken to Brand's office for formal questioning. He spoke broken English and understood all that was said. He was an amazingly self-possessed young man and a thoroughbred, for he politely declined to answer Brand's leading questions. Instead, he smiled, and offered a correction.

"If the Major please," he suggested, "my name is Herr Oberleutnant Hauptmann . . . not Hartmann."

"Thanks," Brand told him dryly. "And now

that we have that correct, how many Fokkers
are there in your unit on this front?"

Herr Hauptmann turned on him his imperturbable smile.

"I have not the slightest idea, Herr Major."

"You're a damned liar," Brand told him, but
there was amusement rather than resentment in
his tone.

The questioning went for nothing. Hauptmann discussed the fighting freely enough and
proved himself an entertaining talker. He was
present at the mess that evening, quite sober in
spite of enormous mixtures of *schnapps* and
French wine. He was sitting in Scott's chair
next to Courtney when Hollister entered the
room. The boy halted rigidly.

"D'you know," Vardon was saying, "when
Scott went out this morning he had on those
zebra-striped pajamas beneath his flying suit?"

Hollister sank into a chair and gulped.

"Fancy," came a voice from up the table,
"going to hell in striped pajamas."

Hollister's body jerked as though he had been
suddenly stabbed. He kept watching Courtney
and the German. Directly Courtney left the
table and went to the blackboard. He reached
for the soiled cloth. His face was distorted beneath a grin. His eyes glittered. He swept the

rag across the names of Woolsey and Cleaver.
He half turned. His voice carried out to the
farthest man.

"I'll never forget Cleaver. He was the one
who had seven—and a half hours . . . the way
he added that half hour."

He turned again to the blackboard. His eyes
lingered on the scrawl that was Scott's name.

"And Doug," he added, "in striped pajamas."

He wiped viciously and left a gray smear on
the board. The rag fell from his fingers.

Down at his distant place Hollister was still
staring. No one paid much attention to him.
All along the table men were forcing their
laughter, drinking as they ate. Vardon pushed
his chair back and burst into that refrain of
bitter humor:

> "Take the cylinders out of my kidneys,
>   Take the scutcheon pins out of my brain;
>   Take the cam-box from under my backbone,
>   And assemble the engine aga-a-i-n."

Herr Oberleutnant Hauptmann burst into
laughter. His pink face grew red. Suddenly,
a chair scraped as Hollister rose. He kicked
backward at it viciously and sprang toward
Courtney, cursing as he ran.

"Stop! Stop it! Merciful God, don't you
know they're dead? Bob . . . and Machen
. . . Cleaver . . . Woolsey . . . Scott! Dead,
I tell you!"

His voice rose to a scream. He stood trembling, with his hands clenched at his sides, the
knuckles white.

"They're not coming back . . . they're dead
. . . and you laugh . . . and sing . . . with the
man who killed . . . Scott!"

He sprang at the startled German.

"You," he cried. "You killed him . . . you
swine!"

He whirled on Courtney.

"And you drink with him . . . and Scott was
your . . . friend!"

His shrill laugh sounded unreal. The room
had become silent.

"You've forgotten him. His murderer is
. . . your friend!"

Courtney left his chair. He moved so swiftly
that Hollister was still standing rigidly with his
hands against his sides when a steel grip closed
on his throat. He was forced backward. His
lungs were cut off.

"You   little   fool! Can't you   understand?"

Suddenly Courtney released him, caught him
as he fell and lifted him up.

"God, I'm sorry, Hollister. You'll learn."

His swift rage had vanished. Hollister, too, was oddly quiet now. He felt his throat tenderly and his head bowed. There were tears in his eyes. Courtney reached out and took his arm.

"Boy, we can't keep thinking. Don't you see we can't? To-morrow's another day. Don't you understand?"

Hollister sobbed. He seized Courtney's hand and held it for an instant, then turned to plunge blindly toward the door. Before he reached it the door was flung open. Framed there, bareheaded and laughing, stood Douglas Scott. A bandage was askew about his temple and in his arms he held an assorted collection of bottles. His tunic was open at the chest to reveal the gay blue and white stripes of a pajama jacket.

"Bon jour, Messieurs. Cheerio!"

He was gleefully drunk. There was a concerted movement toward him. He saw Courtney in the crowd.

"Hello, fellow——"

He patted a bottle affectionately.

"Look—I collected 'em all along the lines. Thought maybe ol' squadron supply ran out 'fore I got home."

Courtney stared at him, then gently took his arm.

"Come in, Doug—to your wake."

Scott laughed uproariously.

"Me dead? Hell, jus' dead drunk, tha's all."

He was surrounded, swept into the room on a wave of relief that lifted their spirits into the heights. Courtney clung to his arm.

"Doug, old man, give it to us. What——"

Scott stared at him owlishly.

"Why, th' motor conked, o' course. I went into a spin . . . naturally. Thought I was a goner . . . 'n then I got th' damned aileron workin' 'n' pancaked into a trench, 's all."

"Where?"

"Damned if I know, Dick. Somewhere. I woke up with a rag around my bean 'n' a stretcher-bearer pourin' good rum down my gullet."

He gazed about from face to face.

"They got plenty good rum up front."

"Not since you left," Courtney suggested.

Scott stared at the bottles he had brought.

"They sent me home on a motorcycle y'understand. We stopped all along th' line an' ever' place we stopped, I got a bottle."

He suddenly found Herr Hauptmann. His eyes widened. Courtney laughed.

"Oh, Doug, this is our enemy-guest, Herr Oberleutnant Hauptmann—the chap who sent you down."

Scott grinned delightedly. He went to the German with his hand extended in gay good humor.

"Glad t' see you, Lieutenant. You got down all right yourself?"

Their hands met.

"Thank you, Herr Scott," he replied in his studied English. "I pancaked, too—in a field with your artillery."

"Good 'nough. Have a drink?"

He seized the nearest filled glass and lifted it above his head.

"Here's to better landing places, fellows."

Hauptmann raised his glass and his eyes twinkled.

"To better luck next time," he offered.

"Same to you."

The others closed in about him, and for the next hour Scott was forced to recount his story, while they drank and joked about the freak of his escape. Courtney listened and his eyes were warm. Hovering near him always, Hollister listened curiously. His eyes were sane again and there was color in his face. When he caught Courtney's eye he smiled. Understanding had come at last.

CHAPTER VII

THE return of Douglas Scott did more to lift
Courtney from his black depression than the
drinking. It was the irrepressible Scott who
discovered that A Flight was relieved of duty in
the morning. He studied the blackboard in-
credulously with eyes that were a little too
dazed to be certain of what they saw.

"I say, Dick," he nodded toward the board,
"is that right, old man? D'y' mean there's no
show this mornin'?"

Courtney chuckled with a spontaneous mirth
that had become strange to him in these few
days with the squadron.

"Quite so. They're saving us for the *pièce
de résistance.*

Scott hesitated thoughtfully. A plan was re-
volving in his brain which suddenly took form.
He rose abruptly.

"In that case, there's an Irish infantryman—
Flaherty—who brought me home. He'll be
somewhere about with his bloomin' cycle. We
can both pile in the side car an' hop back

to Allonville. There's an *estaminet* there, Dick——"

"But what's wrong with our own liquor?"

Scott leaned over him and closed one eye significantly.

"I was thinking of a girl back there—Marie —and another one they called Terese——"

Courtney laughed and stood up. He wanted to be with Scott this night.

"In that case——"

They went out together. Flaherty was seated with a group of sergeant mechanics in the dim yellow light of a hangar. He grinned as they approached him. Scott explained his plan. Flaherty agreed to it without question.

"Whatever you say, sir. The skipper told me to get you back an' I've done it. Whatever happens from now on, sir, is entirely all right with me."

His steady blue eyes were full of humor that was in harmony with his brogue. He parted casually from his acquaintances and led the way to the motorcycle. Courtney and Scott managed to fit themselves in the narrow side car. Flaherty glanced at them from his slightly higher level on the seat.

"All ready, sir?"

At Scott's nod he spun the pedal beneath his hobnailed boot and the engine leaped into noisy action. The machine lurched forward and vanished around a turn beside the hangar. The mechanics saw it last as the side car careened up from the ground on the curve.

The passengers had no opportunity for conversation even had they been so inclined. Flaherty wanted to show a couple of flyers what a dispatch rider could do in the way of speed. He succeeded admirably. They approached a crossroad. The bulky shadows of supply trucks loomed black. A murky opening showed between two of them. Flaherty headed for it and went through.

Scott and Courtney laughed as the screeching of brakes sounded above the staccato firing of the cycle engine. They could not hear the bitter oaths of the truck drivers that followed them into the night and were lost.

There were no lights showing at Allonville, but they could discern the dark silhouettes of squat cottages. Flaherty roared into the village and pulled up with a flourish before a stone building. As the sound of the motor died they heard music and voices drifting out.

"From th' sound of it, sir, this must be the place."

"And the smell," Courtney said.

They sprang to the ground and landed in thick mud. Scott faced the driver.

"Sorry your machine's out of order, Flaherty."

The Irishman stared at him in the darkness.

"But she ain't, sir. She's hittin' on all four an'——"

"Oh, I thought she was limping."

Flaherty grunted as he realized that he was being played with.

"Well," he told them regretfully, "I suppose I'll be goin' on. Th' skipper'll be havin' an attack o' th' fits."

"Oh, to hell with him," suggested Scott. "We'll stake you, Flaherty, if you're broke."

Flaherty shook his head.

"Sorry, sir. Th' only thing that'd give me an excuse would be a crash, 'r somethin'."

"Well, thanks, old man. Good luck."

They shook hands all around. Flaherty glanced back as his machine bucked ahead. In the fleeting instant the handlebar swerved. The cycle turned sharply and headed for a leaning metal lamp-post. It struck with a terrific crash. Flaherty, however, threw one leg over in that spare second and landed running. He wheeled and returned to the two startled flyers. He was grinning.

"Ain't it hell," he rumbled, "just as I was gettin' away t' a fine start?"

Courtney and Scott echoed his laugh.

"Well done, thou good and faithful infantry-man," said Courtney. "Come in and have a spot—or two."

Scott looked at the wrecked machine and was amused. He said: "Flaherty, you'll die in bed—with a priest beside you."

Flaherty returned his gaze soberly.

"I'm hopin' for that, sir, but I doubt it. There ain't enough good fathers t' go round for all of us."

The sound of the crash had brought a little group to the door of the *estaminet*. When they saw that nothing serious had happened they greeted the newcomers with hilarious relief. There were two or three French subalterns among them, some British lieutenants and the girls, Marie and Terese. At least Courtney presumed they were the charmers who had lin-gered in Scott's memory.

"Ah, *Monsieurs, comment allez-vous ce matin?*" one of them called.

Scott laughed back at her.

"Speak in English, Marie. You can."

Courtney observed her blandly. When they went in to mingle with the group he found more to interest him in the picturesque raftered room than in its occupants. He drank cognac and occasionally smiled at some turn in the conver-sation, but he seldom joined it. To himself he admitted that he would rather be back in the squadron bar.

Scott suddenly announced that he was hungry. The bearded old proprietor came forward rubbing his hands.

"Are your eggs fresh?" Scott demanded.

"*Le bon dieu* is my witness, *Monsieur,* this very morning—yesterday morning, I should say —the chickens crowed over my eggs."

"Crowed, or cackled?" Scott asked severely.

The man shrugged and spread expressive hands.

"Ah, *Monsieur,*" his manner was philosophic, "but what does it matter—to a chicken?"

Scott turned to Courtney to find him gravely studying the rafters.

"What is it, old sobersides? Aren't you happy?"

Courtney smiled and shrugged.

"There's nothing new in the act, Doug. I've seen it before, somewhere."

Scott observed him critically and leaned close.

"For God's sake, loosen up, Dick. Forget things—damn it, have a good time."

But when the eggs were brought on and Scott attacked them, Courtney rose lazily and smiled down at him.

"I'm off for a stroll, Doug. Need some air. I'll see you later."

He nodded casually to the others and walked to the door. They watched him in silence, puzzled by his manner. Scott apologized for him.

"He takes the war seriously. He's really the best chap in the world, y'know—just moody—and worried."

The girl called Terese, who was seated nearest the door, detached herself from the group inconspicuously and followed Courtney into the night. Some of the Frenchmen, alert for every play of life about them, saw her maneuver and exchange amused glances. Outside, she saw the dark shadow moving slowly into the gloom and ran in pursuit.

Courtney heard her approaching. He halted and faced about. The girl drew up beside him.

"You are—lonely, *Monsieur?*"

His deep voice was full of quiet amusement when he answered her.

"Not at all, *Mademoiselle.*"

She gazed up at him from large dark eyes that were strangely tragic.

"Do you mind if I walk with you, *Monsieur?*"

"Not if you wish to. I'm not very good company, though."

She moved closer.

"Which way?" he asked.

She shrugged. "Any way you like."

"You have no choice?"

Again her shoulders moved in a gesture of indifference.

"All ways are the same."

Her voice was peculiarly pitched. He was reminded of the verse—"There is a Way, and Ways, and a Way." He smiled grimly.

"You mean they all lead to the same thing?"

She met his gaze steadily. They were moving slowly toward the outskirts of the village.

"Is it not so, *Monsieur?*"

Courtney shook his head deliberately. "No, you're wrong, Terese—you are Terese, aren't you?"

"Yes, I am Terese." She was curious. "But why am I wrong?"

"Because you think all ways are the same. It isn't true—not for a woman. A man may throw himself into the mud—and get up. But a woman can't."

She studied him for a moment in silence.

"You are not like the rest of them—your friend, Scott—all of them.'"

"Oh, yes, I am. I'm worse than any of them."

"But you think a woman can be good—even when there is war."

He laughed.

"Goodness be damned, Terese. I'm not thinking of virtue at all. You misunderstand

me. I simply think we're foolish—all of us who
do things we don't really want to do."

"But what is one to do, *Monsieur?*"

He spoke harshly: "Have a lover, if you
wish. Or have a theory about goodness—but
whatever you have, stick to it. You come to
that—that dive back there—you follow men
into the street? If it makes you happy, all
right. But it doesn't. You don't look happy,
Terese."

She was walking with her head bowed, studying the ground.

"I had a lover, *Monsieur*—we were——"

"Rot," he cut in sharply. "You were to be
married, of course. And he went west. So you
felt so sorry for—yourself, that you——"

Her shoulders moved convulsively as she
choked back a sob. Courtney halted and raised
her face in the cup of his hand. He was
smiling.

"Forget it, Terese. I'm a damned fool."

She controlled her swift emotion and smiled
up at him.

"No, *Monsieur*. You are not—what you say
—'a damned fool.' But I do not onerstan'."

He thought how much her voice sounded like
Major Brand's Celeste.

"There is a girl in England?" she asked, a
little timidly.

"No, Terese. I'm quite alone."

"There is a girl for your friend Scott."

Courtney smiled. "Not that I know of."

Terese nodded her dark head. "Yes, he told me. If he is not killed he will marry her. Meanwhile," she made a gesture with her hand, "he try hard to forget."

Courtney smiled fleetingly. He raised his head at a new note that sounded above the low rumble of the artillery. The lofty sound gained strength.

"Ah." Terese gasped and he saw her face as it grew pale.

He gazed up into the night sky.

"Gothas," he muttered. "A flock of them."

She seized his arm.

"Come, I am afraid."

A siren lifted its brazen voice in the village. They stood close together, strangely fascinated by the heavy drone of the approaching bombers. Another sound cut shrilly into the darkness as a bomb plunged downward in its long arch. Courtney turned swiftly and pushed the girl toward a hayrack in the field beside the road.

"Get under there, Terese."

He stood leaning against the warped frame, while she crouched in the doubtful shelter of the old wagon. When the Gothas swung over,

A First National Picture. The Dawn Patrol.
COURTNEY AND SCOTT ARE BROUGHT TO TASK FOR FLYING OVER THE GERMAN
LINES AGAINST ORDERS.

the night became hideous as they released their charges. It was done swiftly. A lone bomb found its mark in a thacked cottage. The fields were torn and smoking. A very old woman was dead and two fat sows in the kitchen of her cottage were squealing in their death agony. A group of infantrymen postponed their game of cards long enough to draw the body of the crone from the wreckage.

In the acrid gloom Courtney and Terese returned to the *estaminet*. She glanced up at his brooding face curiously.

"You were not frightened, *Monsieur?*"

His lips twitched fleetingly. "They were pretty far away, Terese."

She continued to study his face and was puzzled. This man was something strange in her life and she was peculiarly impressed. Yet she said nothing. They entered the *estaminet* and found most of the group still there. Douglas had vanished. To Courtney's questions the imperturbable Frenchman gestured with his thumb toward the ceiling.

"He went to bed, *Monsieur*. I think he slept through the bombing."

"Doubtless."

Courtney decided that he would be more content at his own quarters than here. He realized, of course, that in his present condition Scott would be better off where he was. He faced the waiting Frenchman.

"Tell him I have gone back. I will see him later this morning."

He turned to the girl.

"*Adieu,* Terese. May your luck be all the best."

She was candidly surprised.

"You are—going, *Monsieur?*"

"Yes."

Her gaze fell beneath his. She did not see the fleet smile that trembled on his lips.

"You see, Terese," he drawled, "I want to claim a distinction. I'd like you to remember me as the one who was different."

She gazed up at him and her sullen eyes were warm.

"It is like that I shall remember, *Monsieur.*"

He bowed and took her hand. He pressed beneath her warm fingers a crisp note and turned swiftly away. The proprietor trotted beside him.

"What became of Flaherty—the Irishman?" Courtney demanded.

The man rolled his eyes in mock reproach.

"Ah, *Monsieur,* he, too, is quite overcome— he sleeps."

Courtney laughed.

"Let him sleep till he awakens. He has a perfect excuse."

He strode out and moved along the cobbled street toward the western edge of the village. Somewhere along the road, he judged, there would be a supply truck, or a dispatch rider, running in his direction. With luck he could get home easily.

Not that it greatly mattered. Vardon's flight would be out with the dawn. At the thought Courtney unconsciously quickened his pace. He found himself wanting to be on the field when the flight came in. He traveled less than a mile before he was hailed by a passing lorry and in this fashion, by a series of transfers along the way, he came upon the familiar airdrome before the morning was very far advanced.

A gray drizzle was falling, cold and dismal. He went unobtrusively to his quarters. For a time he slept. Rising, he took a cold bath, shaved and put on fresh clothing. The uplifting reaction of the night had died and he was again in his customary mood of grim recklessness. He was sipping hot black coffee, brought by an orderly, when the door swung open and Scott plunged into his room.

"What the devil?"

Scott grinned. He wore only the striped

pajama coat above his belt and that was wet and streaked.

"Where's your blouse?" Courtney asked.

"Somebody swiped it, Dick. I woke up an' heard you'd left, so I came, too."

"Well, I'll be damned."

"Righto."

Courtney indicated the bottle of liquor on his table.

"Better have a spot and get off those clothes."

Scott glanced at the coffee.

"That," he said, "when there's—that?" His gaze went to the liquor.

Courtney nodded.

"A bit of variety."

"Oh."

Scott had little time in which to refresh himself. He sprang to the window beside Courtney at the throbbing note of approaching motors, muffled in the thick wet mist of morning. He turned bloodshot eyes skyward, but could see only a blank expanse of gray.

"Four of them, Doug."

"Three gone."

Courtney turned away from the window.

"God!" Scott's voice was pitched low.

They went out on the field. Four planes spiraled down and slithered through the mud.

The pilot of the first ship down half rose in the cockpit and fell back. It was Vardon. They closed in about him. His eyes were glazed and his jaws were clamped.

"Brand," he snarled.

"Come on, we'll take you in to him."

Courtney and Scott helped him to alight and half carried him to the mess room. They did not speak. Vardon was conserving what strength he had for his report to Brand. The major was waiting for him. He stiffened as he saw Vardon between the two others.

"Von Richter moved up—five flights under his command."

Vardon gazed at his superior steadily as he spoke. His voice was strained. There was a momentary silence, charged with the ominous import of his message. Brand moved involuntarily. His face was ghastly in its sudden expression of realization.

"We ran into two flights," Vardon said. "Thoburn—Squires—and Hollister."

Brand recoiled against the bar and attempted a fantastic laugh that failed.

"And you go blighty," he said.

"You'll have to order new crates, sir. Ours are shot to hell."

Brand nodded. He did not look at Vardon, but instead, studied the liquor before him. He seemed to be far away. It was as though the death of three men that morning had left no impression on him. His lips moved queerly.

"Von Richter," he repeated dully.

Suddenly, he took a grip on himself. He glanced swiftly at Vardon.

"All right, old man. We'll get you over to the M.O. Where are you hit?"

Vardon's hand that had been thrust beneath his tunic was slowly withdrawn. It was dripping crimson. It gleamed evilly in the haggard light.

"In the gut," he smiled thinly.

Courtney and Scott held him up between them.

"I'll have a drink before I go." Vardon coughed a little and spat red. "I fancy it'll run out of me before it does any good, though. I feel like a damned sieve."

He tossed off a pony of brandy and they carried him out. Courtney spoke to him.

"Hollister? What about him, Vardon?"

For an instant Vardon regained his old vigor.

"Like a man, by God." He gazed up into Courtney's face. "I saw him zoom—then go out of control. I can swear he was laughing when he passed me."

Courtney lowered his head.

"I'm glad. The kid understood, I fancy—at the finish."

When Vardon at last lay motionless under an opiate awaiting the ambulance, they turned silently away. He was badly hit. They did not expect to see him again. Courtney and Scott walked back toward the mess room. Others followed them through the cold rain. Somewhere in the drab void high over the drome a plane was circling. The sound increased and Courtney halted.

"He's diving."

The plane continued to plunge with the power on until it flashed into their range of vision. They saw at once that it was a Roland, carmine-striped. There was an instant's startled delay. As the ship flattened away an object hurtled from the cockpit and the pilot waved. Courtney sprang ahead as it became certain that the falling object was not a bomb.

The German was zooming into the dun-colored sky when he stooped over a pair of field boots, bound together. There was a note attached by a length of wire. He read it swiftly: "Ground boots for the use of English flying officers."

He laughed and passed the message to Scott.

"We can use them," he said, examining the boots.

A young pilot reached out for them, as though to carry out some suddenly determined plan. Courtney gently pushed him back.

"Never mind, I'll keep them."

The enemy plane had brought Major Brand from his office. He had watched the play, and now, with swift realization of the effect it would have on his men, he strode in among them.

"One moment, gentlemen." He gazed coolly at the circle of set faces.

"I think I understand, but it can't be done. There will be no voluntary patrols unless I order them."

His gaze hesitated on Courtney.

"Von Richter's squadron is the best of the lot. We've got all we can handle as a combination. Is that clear, gentlemen? No informal strafing."

He pivoted abruptly and walked away. Scott was studying the worn boots in Courtney's hand. His resentment brought a scowl to his face and when he looked up at Courtney, some understanding passed between them. Scott, instead of going on to the bar, strode obliquely toward the hangars. Courtney, still clinging to the boots, fell into step with him.

Scott said: "To hell with him, Dick. We've got to do something about these damned boots."

It was to him an insult, as though an opponent on the polo field had belittled his team; no more than that. The grim element of death did not enter into his calculations, or the traditional law of discipline. With Courtney it was somewhat the same, except that he understood the matter of discipline and of death, but chose to disregard them. Both of them thought of it now as a sporting thing and as they drew into the shelter of the first hangar, Scott voiced his plan.

"We've got to give 'em some sort of an answer, Dick. If we make it good enough, Brand can't do anything very well."

Courtney nodded thoughtfully.

"He'll do enough, though, if we get a setback."

Scott smiled knowingly.

"Come through, fellow. You had the same idea at the same instant. I saw it in your eye."

Courtney laughed.

"Something of the sort," he admitted.

He drew a notebook from his pocket and a pen. Using a workbench for a desk, he scrawled a note, while Scott read it eagerly over his shoulder. It was addressed to Count Herman von Richter.

"You'll need them on the retreat to Germany," he wrote.

"Bravo," Scott nodded his approval. "We can drop that in the boots right on their door-step——"

"Along with some other little gifts."

"Righto."

They set about immediately to inspect their Bristols and from the ammunition supply they took sufficient bombs to fill their improvised racks. It was simple to win the help of the mechanics.

"If any questions are asked," Scott told them severely, "just say you're priming these crates for to-morrow's flight."

"Good enough, sir."

"No fuss," Courtney added. "We'll cat-eye our way off the drome when the rest of them are taking on rum."

"Right, sir. We'll tow the planes just be-fore you're ready."

The sergeant paused doubtfully.

"What'll I say to the major after you take off, Captain?"

Courtney grunted.

"Go to bed before we get away. Get out of sight. That'll relieve you of any charge of collusion."

"Very good, sir. Good luck to you both."

The sergeant of mechanics gazed curiously at the boots that lay on a petrol drum.

"Might I ask, sir, what do you intend to do with them?"

Courtney chuckled.

"Returning them to their rightful owner."

The man grinned and with his assistants began a studied grooming of the ships that lay in the gloom of the hangar. Courtney and Scott attended to the loading of ammunition belts and watched while the tanks were filled with petrol. When they were satisfied that nothing more could be done they waved cheerfully to the mechanics and went back to the bar.

It would not be difficult to withdraw from the mess-room gathering later. They were exulting in the inner security of a vast confidence when they joined their fellows in the bar.

CHAPTER VIII

THE dreary day was drenched in steady rain that left misery in the lines. The air was deserted and there was quiet all along the front. The outposts huddled in their slimy stations just north of the woods called Bois de Dames and on to Lens; beyond that to Vimy Ridge and thence to Arras. The artillery was spasmodic on both sides and the infantry cursed vilely in the muck. It was the sort of a day which the line commands would report as quiet.

In Allonville Forest the pines were dripping. In the gray melancholy light of afternoon the First Squadron lay sprawled in bunks, or followed the usual custom of steady drinking. No one noticed the little group of mechanics who wheeled two planes to the distant end of the airdrome. Or, if they did, there was nothing out of the ordinary in the scene. Neither were Courtney and Scott missed in the squadron bar.

They went up to their places without comment. Except for two mechanics, the others dissolved in the gray mist. Voices were muffled.

"Contact!"

The signal repetition sounded hollowly and the motors coughed, caught the sparks and burst into full-throated song. The mechanics stepped swiftly aside and, turning, vanished into the twilight. The planes went into the wind through mud and water, rocking crazily. Courtney pulled up and raised his hand to Scott. As he gazed over the side he could make out shadowy figures running. He grinned as one emerged from the headquarters office, waving his arms. It was Brand.

He climbed steeply to get over the trees. Scott hung on close. Vision was blurred, and even the forest below had become a treacherous gray, no different from the rest of the earth. A blanket of mist intervened between them and the ground, so that it would be necessary to venture low to get their bearings.

Courtney studied his map. They had the advantage of a tail wind, so long as they headed east over the British lines. But when they swung into the north it quartered them. He was counting on the rain to muffle their approach. Moreover, he told himself, they would have the double advantage of surprise. No gun crew would be expecting them. He kicked the left rudder to bank sharply to the north.

The two planes bored into the metallic sky

on a northward course for seven minutes. Courtney watched his instrument panel. Infrequently he half turned to see that Scott was following. They were doing an air speed of a hundred and forty miles an hour and his chart indicated the airdrome should be sixteen kilometers back. He wiggled the ailerons and went down obliquely. Scott roared down on his tail.

When they flattened off in the confusing dull mist there were only fields beneath them. They promptly idled the power and circled. Suddenly Scott opened his throttle in signal and pointed west. Courtney had a glimpse of his arm as he swept it in a gesture ahead. Beyond them a low ground swell formed a shallow bowl in the center of which lay the drome.

The hangars, long and narrow, partly concealed beneath a camouflage of tree limbs, lay at the far end. As he swept down Courtney saw men running through the rain. A line of planes was drawn up precisely nose to nose. Back along the edge of the 'drome were the quarters.

Courtney sent his roaring Bristol low over the enemy ships. At the head of the line he flung the boots over and promptly released his first bomb. He was too low for timing. He laughed savagely as the missile ripped a Roland in a burst of fiery destruction. Scott was planting his bombs over the hangars.

A machine gun was spitting angry orange streaks upward at an oblique. Courtney shoved the stick forward and dived over it, spraying the crew with his Lewis. He saw two of them sprawl. The others parted and ran. He centered the controls and circled back, releasing a burst over the officers' quarters. Far up the field he saw Scott raking the Rolands on a long plunge.

As he banked around to attack the hangars once more, he swept the drome with a roving gaze that caught the movement about two planes. They sped out across the field. Courtney dived down over them as the first one left the ground. He saw distinctly the face of the pilot as he tripped the trigger. The rising plane quivered, hung for an instant and fell back on its tail. When he banked around to turn a burst upon the second, the wreckage below was in flames. He trained the Lewis on the second plane full into the cockpit. It, too, keeled over and crashed.

Another blaze sprang up hungrily on his right. The hangars were burning. A dull explosion sent up a cloud of sparks and he felt his plane jerk and settle in the current. Another machine gun was spurting toward him from the line of burning planes. He stared around for Scott and found him rising and diving like a desperate kingfisher over his quarry.

Courtney flattened off fifty yards away and signaled. Scott loosed a final burst upon the burning quarters, then roared after him. They climed into the south rapidly. A minute's flight brought them suddenly over a captive balloon rising for observation.

Courtney grunted. He pictured the scene below, subconsciously. They had heard the commotion at the drome, or perhaps a swift telephone message before the wires went out. They were raising the sausage in signal, probably a relay message to the infantry. In the moment that he dived on the helpless balloon Scott swept down beside him. He saw the flashing laugh as their guns spoke together.

The wrinkled bag seemed to quiver before it became a mass of flames. The ground crew on the truck below sprang away. Some of them went down beneath the burning folds of the bag. Courtney pointed up, and a hundred feet behind him Scott turned deliberately to stare back upon the confusion they had created. A Vickers was spitting oblique tongues of flames straight at them from a sheltered nest.

Courtney stiffened as his motor stalled. The stench of hot oil mingled in his nostrils with the reek of powder and the acrid smell of petrol. In the sudden lull of silence he heard Scott's engine droning evenly. He was still so close to the ground that he could hear, too, the rattle of the Vickers. He stared over and saw little round holes appearing in the wings.

He reached for the pump. The motor stubbornly refused. He promptly centered the controls and studied the field below for the best landing. His eyes beneath the goggles were peculiarly quiet and his lips were oddly smiling. He raised his left hand in signal to Scott.

Mechanically then, Courtney jockeyed the controls and watched the gray earth swiftly rising. He made the landing mechanically and in the same detached fashion sprang to the ground, watching Scott. He waved in signal that he was unhurt and swept his arm in a gesture that was intended to send him on his way.

But Scott had a different notion. From the woods at the distant edge of the stubble field a group of Germans was approaching on the run. Scott jerked his little Bristol up on its tail, came down in a spin, and as he flattened off, dived for the surprised runners. Courtney bent hurriedly over his ship with a match. A wad of oil-soaked waste caught the flame. He stepped back as it spread.

As he wheeled, prepared to fight it out with his automatic, a strange sight brought a terse oath from his lips. Scott was pointing down to land. His motor was idled and he was leaning far over the side. As his wheels touched the ground and bumped roughly through the mud, he beckoned. Courtney sprang toward him.

"Get out of it, you fool."

Scott's lips moved and he was laughing. Behind him the Germans were coming on, shooting as they ran. The dry thin whine of bullets was like a wind through a crevice. Courtney pulled himself up on the wing, close to the cockpit. Scott opened the throttle and the overladen Bristol lurched ahead. It rose drunkenly and lumbered into the air. The Germans had halted and were firing methodically.

Courtney waved at them mockingly. The ship jerked in a down current. He turned swiftly. Scott was staring straight ahead. His teeth were clamped on his lower lip. His face was oddly gray, like the mist about them. Courtney saw a crimson stain spreading like red ink on a blotter on the shoulder of Scott's tunic. The boy turned his head and smiled. He nodded reassuringly.

He bent down to work the controls. The
Bristol was refusing to climb. It was flying in
the manner of a bird with a wounded wing.
Ahead of them below the nose the twisting scar
of the German second-line trenches ran a zig-
zag course east and west. The grayness down
there had red and yellow tongues that leaped
upward.

Courtney clung to the wing. He kept watching Scott's face. Now and then he turned his
gaze to the wings. New holes were there like
staring dead eyes each time he looked. He understood instantly when a bullet hit the oil line.
He saw the spurt of dark liquid that spread
over Scott's face. The plane dived, straightened again and climbed. The engine was turning over, but without much effect.

They passed over the second line and went
on. Scott was low in the cockpit, fighting to
stretch the glide across the grim terrain to
British ground. For a little while, in his help-
lessness, Courtney was strangely eager to live.
He did not, of course, analyze his emotion. He
was scarcely aware of his· own voice as he
called to the man at the controls, only to have
his words swept away on the rush of wind.

"Pull out, fellow. We're in a right-hand
spin—center—easy on the stick—that's the
stuff!"

Scott, working on his own instinct, was ma-
neuvering the careening plane exactly as
Courtney was so crazily directing. They were
suddenly heading down on a long oblique toward the friendly lines. The rifle fire from the
German first trenches rippled after them. A
hundred yards beyond the ragged ditch a shell
hole dipped its crater into the earth. Scott
saw it, but the Bristol was out of control now.
They nosed straight down. Courtney started
to leap, but he was flung aside. He crashed into
thick mud. The plane buried its nose and the
undercarriage splintered.

Scott, pinned in the cockpit, made no effort
to save himself. He lay back motionless, staring up into the thin rain. Courtney, dazed for
a fleeting instant, straightened and plunged toward him. From the trench half a dozen
Frenchmen in soiled horizon blue, sprang back
to help them.

Their shouted warnings, made emphatic by
gesticulations, were unnecessary. Courtney
knew that the enemy fire would be coming over.
He lifted Scott from the shattered cockpit. A
French sergeant appeared beside him. The
man seemed to sense the approaching shell. He
struck swiftly at Courtney's arm and went
down flat on his belly. Courtney dropped be-

side him, shielding the limp body in his arms
with his own.

The shell screamed with a tortured sound and
fell a dozen yards from the wrecked Bristol.
A shower of débris spattered upon the motionless men. Courtney spat and smiled at the
Frenchman.

"Thanks."

They rose and went on. Another shell
shrieked its warning as they plunged back into
the trench. An officer thrust a pint flask into
Courtney's hand. He nodded and poured the
liquor between Scott's teeth. The boy coughed
and opened his eyes. He smiled faintly.

"Thanks, fellow. I'll come around."

Courtney up-ended the bottle again. This
time Scott helped him, consciously swallowing.
He stirred and now his eyes were less dazed.

"Damned good stuff they have up here,
Dick."

Courtney, kneeling, was cutting away his
sleeve at the shoulder. He stared at the
wound. A Vickers slug had torn away the
flesh from front to back.

"You lost some beef," Courtney said.

Scott grinned.

"Sure. An' a little broth. I got washed out
for a minute—all right now."

He straightened and sank back. The loss of blood had weakened him.

Raw iodine from a first-aid kit brought him up stiffly. But when a bandage was bound smoothly over the wound he laughed and got to his feet.

"Where in hell are we?" he demanded.

A French captain smiled grimly and told him.

"Can we get back to a motor?"

The captain shrugged.

"Communication lines."

"Good enough. Thanks."

They ducked involuntarily as a shell rumbled over. It exploded behind the trench. Courtney went up on the parapet and stood for an instant.

"There goes Brand's little Bristol," he called down.

Scott laughed and reached up with his good arm to draw him into shelter.

"Come on, fellow, let's take our hell where we find it."

They parted from the curious Frenchmen and weaved a retreat over uncertain duckboard by way of the communications. At the second line they were recognized instantly, for reports of their flight already had been sent back from the outpost telephone. Eager questions in French and broken English were fired at them with staccato speed.

Courtney gave them laconic replies and asked for a motor.

"To be sure, *Monsieur*." An elderly lieutenant led them to his captain, and he in turn communicated by telephone with the colonel. They were escorted to the road, where presently a low motor car, thickly coated with mud, whirled up before them. In the front seat were a driver and a poilu.

The driver saw that Scott was wounded.

"It will be rough going, sir."

"Hit the gun," said Scott. "I'm all right."

The car lurched on the road. The rear end whipped crazily as it slithered in the mud. Courtney and Scott clung to their seats, forgetful again of the existence of discipline and death. They drank in deep breaths of the damp air and lifted their faces to the cold exhilarating rain. They made no attempt to talk. The men in front were likewise silent, intent on the road ahead.

When the car whirled into the familiar road through the pines of Allonville, Courtney straightened. He spoke for the first time in miles.

"Brand will break me, Doug."

"Both of us."

But Courtney shook his head.

"No, I think not. He's been after me for this sort of thing. Now he's got enough to crash me."

Scott chuckled.

"He may recommend it, fellow. But we've got verification of the drome attack. The Frenchmen up there saw the blaze, y'know."

The car halted abruptly with a grinding of brakes. The door of the office opened to cast a flood of yellow light in an oblong patch. Bathurst was peering out at them. His eyes widened when he recognized them. He stepped out quickly and spoke to Courtney.

"The major wants you, Dick." He wagged his head regretfully. "You shouldn't have done it."

"What about me?" Scott leaned forward to study his face.

Bathurst shook his head again.

"No. It's Courtney he wants."

Courtney laughed without humor. He thanked the Frenchmen quietly and waved an ironic salute to Scott.

"We who are about to die salute you," he quoted.

He followed Bathurst into the office. Brand's back was turned to them as he paced the floor. He was in his trousers and undershirt. His hair was rumpled and his hands were thrust into his pockets. The bottle on his desk was half empty. Cigarette stubs littered the floor, and his blouse and gear were lying heaped in a corner. He whirled as the door closed.

He stared at Courtney briefly.

"Get out, Bathurst." His voice rasped.

Courtney met his gaze levelly. They were separated by perhaps a yard of littered plank floor.

"You wanted to see me?" Courtney's tone was steady.

Brand was silent for a moment. His blood-shot eyes glittered strangely in the light and the muscles beneath his unshaved jaws moved jerkily.

"You are under arrest, Courtney."

He managed to say that and control his voice.

"Yes?"

The cool insolence broke the major's resolve.

"Yes, damn you. Direct disobedience." He shouted now and his hands were clenching and opening as though he were struggling against the impulse to strike this man before him.

"Court-martial," he barked. "Conduct un-becoming an officer and a—gentleman."

His laugh was a snarl.

"A gentleman," he repeated.

He moved up two paces and his face was within as many inches of Courtney's.

"A damned drunkard," he spat. "You were drunk when you went out."

"You're a damned liar, Brand."

The major drew back. His flushed face turned yellowish. His throat muscles rippled, but he did not speak. He swallowed twice and controlled himself. It was a magnificent effort.

"If I struck you, Courtney, you could whine to a court-martial."

They stood rigidly. Courtney's slow smile was cruel.

"If you struck me," he drawled, "I couldn't whine to a court-martial, Brand. I'd kill you —and call up G.H.Q. for a new C.O."

The threat was without melodrama. Courtney's voice was cool, argumentative, but without heat. Its very calmness made it deadly. It had the effect of giving Brand a new grip on himself.

"I know what your defense will be. They telephoned. You were crafty enough to fly up the line for identification, weren't you?"

Courtney smiled.

"I figured on the tail wind." He was no longer angry.

Brand gazed at him. In the silence there they were both conscious of the alarm clock.

"We're ordered out after Von Richter in the morning." Brand spoke dully, as though to himself. "You and Scott crippled 'em. That will go in your favor, of course."

"I'll deny we went to the drome if you wish. We can leave that part out."

The casual tone brought into Brand's haggard eyes the swift gleam of disbelief.

"You mean that?"

"Of course."

Brand was silent again, thoughtful. He looked straight at Courtney.

"Why?"

Courtney laughed.

"I'd tell any lie to get out of this command, Brand. I want to get away from you kid-butchers."

It was, for an electric instant, as though he had struck the major between the eyes. Brand reeled back and flung out his hand for support on the desk. With the other he wiped a red mist from before his eyes. He nodded. Words choked him.

"All right, Courtney. Get out. I'm going to break you—break you out of the air service, d'you understand?"

The tall figure in the half-light stood motionless. Deep shadows cut lines in his jowls and his cheeks were hollows carved deep in relief.

It was Courtney's turn to control himself. He managed it. He even forced a smile.

"Go as far as you like, Brand." He turned away abruptly.

"Wait."

When he faced Brand again the major was pouring a drink into a glass that shook.

"What about Scott? Did he come out of it?"

Courtney nodded.

"He has a flesh wound. We lost both the crates."

He started toward the door and paused.

"If you can find it in you," he said deliberately, "I wish you'd recommend the kid. He landed under enemy fire to pick me up. Otherwise I should have saved you all the red tape of a court-martial."

He chuckled bitterly.

"Unless," he added, "you object to giving these boys anything more than sure death."

Brand moved toward him impulsively. The telephone buzzed. He halted.

"Wait, Courtney."

He picked up the receiver and barked his station. A voice came raspingly.

"What's that? . . . I say, what do you mean?" Brand's hand was shaking so that the instrument danced crazily before him. His voice trembled. The distant voice repeated itself.

"Oh . . . quite so, Colonel . . . yes . . . very well. Thank you, sir."

The telephone fell from his hand. He leaned against the desk and began to laugh. Tears trickled from his eyes like drops of blood from which the color had been drained.

"Courtney, by God . . . I congratulate you. I do, so help me."

His laughter rose shrilly and he rushed across the room to pick up his soiled garments. He shrugged into the blouse and reached up to a hook for his stick. With another gesture he put on his cap and slapped his boots with the stick.

"Have a drink, Courtney—you poor damned fool. Have a drink."

Courtney, with his hand still gripping the door knob, was staring at him. He moved back into the room and his voice changed.

"I'm sorry, Brand. I didn't realize you were—drunk."

Brand burst into laughter.

"Drunk, eh?"

He poured the single glass to the brim and handed it over to Courtney. He raised the bottle in a gesture to his own lips.

"To Major Richard Courtney, commanding the First Squadron!"

"What?"

Brand tipped the bottle and emptied it. He set it down deliberately and wiped his lips with the back of his hand.

"Righto, my lad. Headquarters just ordered me up to Wing Nine. I'm to appoint my successor . . ." he laughed insanely and flung the bottle against the wall ". . . and I've appointed . . . you!"

The bottle crashed and splintered. Brand lurched from the room. Courtney stood motionless, staring at the untouched liquor in his glass.

CHAPTER IX

He remained there like a grotesque shadow
for a long minute. He heard Brand speaking
to Bathurst in the office outside. His words
were unintelligible to Courtney, but the voice
was drunken. It broke frequently to give way
to a chortle. Somewhere in one of the hangars
the mechanics were testing a motor. When
they idled it the dull reverberation of the far-
off guns was faint and almost gentle, like summer thunder. The clock ticked.

Courtney set the glass down untouched. He
licked his dry lips and reached for a cigarette.
He lit it and gazed about the room. His nostrils quivered slightly at the stench. Stale
liquor and smoke, damp clothing . . . oil and
petrol . . . a trace of powder . . . that must
have been in his own garments.

A whisky bottle that had been used for a
candlestick clung to the desk in the muck of its
own making. The edge of the desk showed
little black parallel burns where Brand had allowed his cigarettes to lie. In the corner lay a

heap of soiled underwear, woolen socks, an old pair of field boots.

Courtney thought: I must clean this place out. It stinks. It's not fit for a man. There's no excuse for the filth. It's like a white man letting himself go native in Africa. It's a rotten thing to do.

Brand returned to him abruptly. He flourished a sheet of official paper.

"Until your commission arrives, Major, this will do."

Courtney took the paper and glanced at it. Bathurst had typed to Brand's dictation. It was merely official notification of his temporary promotion.

"Thanks."

Brand laughed.

"I'm leaving you the command, Courtney— the château—and the little baggage you seemed to like so well—all of it."

"You're generous."

"I can afford to be."

Courtney sat down in the major's chair. An ironic smile gave his face a fleeting mellowness in the light.

"It will be difficult for me to take your place, Brand. I'm not the type."

Brand laughed brutally.

"You're damned well right it will be difficult.

A First National Picture.

The Dawn Patrol.

DEATH BECKONS ALL WHO ANSWER THE CALL OF THE " DAWN PATROL."

You'll know what it is to send kids out—when you can't go yourself. What it——"

"Why can't I go myself?"

Brand stared at him.

"Because, you blithering ass, G.H.Q. won't stand for it. Don't you suppose I'd have been out——"

Courtney shrugged.

"Then I'll probably take my court-martial after all."

Brand observed him with bitter humor in his eyes.

"Perhaps, but I won't be bothered to make out the charges. I'll be——"

"What are you doing with the Ninth, Brand?"

"Taking over the command. And I'll always have first crack at trained replacements—and I won't ever need them as often, or as many of them, as you will every week."

"I dare say."

"You'll learn."

Courtney remembered when he had said those words to Hollister. He nodded. His troubled gaze went straight to Brand. He spoke evenly.

"I probably will," he admitted. "I've got it coming to me. I know you think I'm all sorts of a rotter, but it wasn't that. I——"

Brand leaned over the desk impulsively. Now his own eyes were suddenly friendly and his voice was gentle.

"Not at all, Courtney, old man. I understand. I've understood all along. It's been hell for me—it'll be hell for you. It's war."

Courtney bowed his dark head for an instant. He stood up and extended his hand. Brand took it in his own.

"Good luck, Brand. I'm glad we got around to this, finally. It clears the air."

"So am I, Courtney. Best of luck—and tell the boys good-by for me."

As he wheeled and started toward the door the telephone sounded angrily. There was a moment's hesitation. Brand grinned.

"Snap it at 'em, Major."

Courtney recovered himself and took up the instrument. He spoke curtly.

"Thirty-first Squadron . . . yes, this is the C.O. . . . what's that?"

The voice buzzed like a harried dragon fly.

"Hell, you're not talking to Brand," he cut in. "This is Courtney, acting C.O. I took that damned plane out myself . . . yes . . . with Scott."

The rasping burst upon his ear again.

"Very well, Colonel. I'm sorry. There'll be no more solo flights."

Brand came back to the desk. He tapped his boot leg with his stick triumphantly.

"The old brass hat was giving me hell for your flight, wasn't he, Courtney?"

"He was."

Brand chuckled and, waving his stick, retreated.

"I'll send for my gear," he called back.

Courtney bent over the heaped papers on the desk. The topmost sheet bore Brand's handwriting. He read his own name . . . squadron commander, acting major . . . the remnants of A Flight . . . Scott, flight commander . . . Selfridge . . . Galloway. B Flight was shattered, lacking even Vardon's name.

"Bathurst."

The adjutant appeared in the door, smiling.

"Send up for a quart of brandy, will you?"

"Righto, Major. And by the way, congratulations."

Courtney nodded. He commenced to sort the papers and straighten the litter on his desk. When he opened the top drawer he found a heap of flimsy copies of old orders. He shuffled through them. They bore familiar names . . . Parker, Willoughby, Wentworth . . . nearly all of the men already gone. There were copies of letters to mothers and widows signed originally by Brand.

"God," Courtney muttered, "that's part of the damned job, too."

Beneath the papers he came upon empty flasks and finally an unsealed envelope. He could feel some object inside. He withdrew the medal and the striped ribbon of the *Croix de Guerre,* inscribed to Brand. He grunted.

That, of course, must be sent on along with the other things . . . the old underwear, he thought, and grinned ironically.

Having a similar decoration himself, along with a collection of others, Courtney knew its worth. His smile was not at Brand, but at the memory of a hairy French general who had kissed him on both cheeks before a whole division. He could think of that while he worked in the confusion.

Bathurst came in with the brandy. Courtney handed him the greasy glass that stood on the desk.

"Either have that boiled out, or get me a new one, will you, old man?"

Bathurst raised the glass to the light and smiled wryly.

"I don't blame you, Dick."

The familiar name did not strike a jarring note on Courtney's ear. He had not yet seriously considered his new title and would never so consider it in the ordinary course of events.

When he was burrowing through other drawers of the desk, assembling official material in one stack, gathering Brand's effects in another, the telephone called him again.

"You will put out two full flights at dawn," came the abrupt command, after they had established identification. "The infantry is about demoralized. Von Richter's circus is ripping hell out of the lines."

"I understand, Colonel, but it can't be done. I haven't got two full flights." In his own mind he added: "Only a few kids full of liquor and fear."

"You're getting four replacements, Major."

"Four," Courtney repeated dully. "Probably cadets, aren't they? You expect me to put out two flights against Von Richter?"

"That's the order."

Courtney shrugged in futility. He tried again

"It's murder, Colonel. These replacements are boys. They won't have a shadow of a chance."

"Sorry, Major. There's nothing else to do about it."

He leaned over the instrument and his voice suddenly changed. A gentle pleading note crept into it to take the place of the harsh obstinacy.

"All right, Colonel, but may I ask a special order, sir?"

The silence that met this encouraged him.

"If I can lead the flight, Colonel——"

"No, absolutely not, Courtney. We can get replacements, but experienced men are scarce. Stick to your job."

The clicking sound of a distant lost connection snapped in Courtney's ear. He bent over the papers again, studying the blanks that remained to be filled in each flight. Bathurst came in with the clean glass. Courtney poured a drink and looked up moodily.

"Bring your glass in, Bathurst."

The adjutant went out to his desk and returned. Courtney pushed the brandy toward him.

"We've got to put out two flights," he droned.

Bathurst paused with his drink poised halfway to his lips. He shook his head.

"It's no use, is it?"

Courtney growled an oath. He rose nervously and went to the window.

"Fancy, Bathurst. They expect us to stop Von Richter."

His hand was trembling when he lit a cigarette.

"I'm the executioner now. I begin to under-

stand Brand already. It's funny, isn't it?"
He laughed bitterly.

"Someone has to send them out."

Courtney chewed on his under lip. The sleepless hours and the strain showed in his eyes. His muscles were beginning to twitch oddly, too, and the skin over his cheek bones was drawn taut. He looked old.

"It's a thankless job," Bathurst said dully.

"Thankless." Courtney's growl was savage. "Damn thanks. It's inhuman. To sit here and wait—tear your guts out—wonder what's happening to them—and knowing it."

He reached for the bottle. Scott sauntered in, feigning nonchalance.

"Are my ears correct?" He chuckled. "Am I to salute and call you major?"

Courtney gulped his brandy and set the glass down. He smiled wearily.

"Quite so, Doug. I'm a god now, with a little brass hat."

Scott became serious. He looked at the bottle.

"Aren't you—hitting the stuff pretty hard, fellow?"

Courtney's humor snapped.

"What the hell of it?"

He saw the swift hurt in Scott's face and was sorry.

"Forgive me, Doug. I'm a bit jumpy."

Scott laughed and was relieved.

"Righto. I'm taking the jumps myself, old dear. Y'see, Brand just told me I'm leading A Flight."

"Yes, God bless you."

Scott laughed. There was actual happiness in the sound.

"I'll miss you though, Dick. I'll be wishing I could ride on your tail in rear position."

Courtney smiled wearily. A field sergeant interrupted them. He saluted and turned a troubled gaze on Courtney.

"The replacements are in, sir."

"Transfers?" Scott asked.

"Transfers hell," snarled Courtney. "More boys." He nodded to Scott. "Take care of them, won't you? Thanks."

He was left alone. He had seized upon the opportunity to avoid that first contact with the youngsters. It would come soon enough and he dreaded it. There would be the hypocrisy of stern discipline . . . the tight-lipped instructions . . . the silly twaddle about glorious patriotism. His lips curled scornfully. He thought of those meaningless phrases which pedagogic minds had implanted in immature brains . . . "For God, for country, and for

king"; and that silliest of all inanities, credited
properly or not to the American, Decatur: "Our
country, right or wrong."

He grunted and was not aware that he spoke
half aloud. "Our general staff," he para-
phrased, "right or wrong."

He drank a lonely sardonic toast in the pun-
gent cognac of France.

It occurred to him that he wanted to have a
talk with Scott about the next patrol. He preferred that it be informal, as one flight leader
to another rather than from commanding officer to subordinate. He left the office and
headed for Scott's quarters.

There was no response to his knock and he
entered. The room was in disorder. That was
not unusual, but Courtney was mildly surprised
by the sight of an extra trunk thrown in the
center of the floor. Extending from its place
beneath the cot, Doug's trunk was carelessly
open. He glanced at it and was quietly amused.
Suddenly his eyes widened and he stiffened
abruptly.

On top of the clothing in Scott's trunk a
framed portrait lay face up. He saw that it
was a picture of Lady Mary Cambridge. He
stood rigidly staring down at the familiar face.
His eyes misted and the carved lines in his face

grew taut, then relaxed. He smiled and turned away.

She had not given Scott the verse about the high soul and the low, he thought. Perhaps, he reminded himself bitterly, Scott was one of those men who could choose the way his soul should go. He wheeled and left the room heavily. His shoulders drooped faintly and wrinkles creased the cloth of his coat against his wide flat back. It was as if his body had shriveled oddly in a moment when age overtook him.

His feet paced mechanically toward the mess room. He raised his head and turned sharply to his own quarters. Somehow he did not want to face Scott just then. He would have to think it out for a while. Get himself together. Queer. Damned queer.

His mind kept running along like something apart from himself. . . .

. . . Of all the men in England, Douglas Scott. Strange that Doug hadn't mentioned her . . . he must have known . . . she would have told him . . . they would correspond . . . she must be aware at this minute that he and Scott were together . . . in the same squadron . . . hitting it off together.

Courtney stumbled over his own doorsill and into his quarters. He flung off his outer cloth-

ing and sank into a chair. With an effort he
rounded up his straying thoughts that scattered
in a dozen channels. . . .

Come now, it's nothing to bother about. It's
just one of those impossible coincidents that
are never permitted in fiction because they
happen so regularly in life. Nothing unusual
about it, really. Lady Mary and Doug were
bound to meet in London. Most natural thing
on earth for him to tumble head over heels in
love with her and she with him. . . .

God, she must love him, too, because she accepted him as he was. No admonitions . . . no
fuss about his failings . . . no silly verse to be
set up before him like a blooming flowered
motto on the wall. That was the real thing
when a woman accepted a man as he was.
When they tried to shellac his morals and re-
form his conduct generally they were either
mothers, or maiden aunts, or merely curious
females playing with a specimen.

Courtney squirmed in his chair. His grin
was a grotesque mockery. He went to his trunk
and brought out the portrait to set it before him
on the table. A whisky bottle stood beside it.
He laughed aloud. The calm face of Lady
Mary seemed to gaze at him reproachfully.

She might be standing there before him in the
flesh. She had been reproachful so very often.

He remembered that she had said if it were not
for her love she would scarcely try to change
him over. He shook his head in silent protest.

Love didn't change over the thing to which it
gave itself. Only a great and overwhelming
curiosity could do that. It would be disastrous
to love. If such a course were possible, a woman would suddenly find herself with a man
entirely different from the one her love had
altered. What then?

He recalled that Mary had said once:

"Dick, you lack stability. You're too light-
hearted. It's a lovable quality, but life has its
serious moments. You're too easily swayed by
the emotion of the moment."

He laughed again and it sounded strange in
his ears. He still lacked stability, he admitted,
but she could not accuse him now of light-heart-
edness. Nor could she find any argument with
him over life's seriousness. He wondered if he
was still swayed by the emotion of the moment.
He decided that he was not. The thought
brought him around to himself and his immedi-
ate moment. He would prove that here was one
emotion and one moment which would not sway
him in the least.

He wrapped his faded dressing gown about
him and started toward the bar. Halfway he

met Scott and a companion approaching him. Scott called out.

"I say, Dick, see who's here."

He gazed at the slim figure beside Scott and drew up.

"Merciful God." His exclamation came softly. "It's Gordon . . . Gordon Scott."

The boy sprang out to take his hand.

"Dick."

He stared up into the seamed face and was suddenly embarrassed.

"Oh, I beg pardon." He stood stiffly and saluted.

Courtney drew him closer, smiling.

"Forget it, Gordon. I—I was surprised, that's all. Why, you don't belong here—not yet."

"Of course I do. I've been raising hell trying to get my send-off."

Scott was stern-faced. He glanced at his brother swiftly and then to Courtney.

"Good God, Dick, he's a schoolboy."

"Yes." Courtney looked at the youngster. "I thought you were in school, Gordon."

"I was," the tone was proud. "But I chucked it—and enlisted. Went through ground school in four weeks—you thought I was a kid."

He faced Douglas.

"Yes," his brother said slowly, "I did. But you're a man now."

A glance passed between him and Courtney that was full of meaning. It did not escape the boy.

"If you birds think you're going to treat me like a boarding-school brat you're wrong— major or not." He laughed up at Courtney. "I passed the combat test—with honors."

Courtney nodded.

"Of course. Don't you worry, Gordon. We haven't got any silver trays about the place to carry you on. It's potluck in this outfit, you'll find."

"Fine."

Courtney looked at Douglas.

"I dropped in at your place—it was Gordon's traps I saw, then?"

"Yes. I put him in there temporarily. Just took him over to the mess for a spot."

The brothers observed Courtney's dressing gown and smiled together.

"You're heading there yourself," Douglas accused him.

"Yes. I got sick of drinking alone."

"You shouldn't do it, old man." Scott dropped a hand on his arm affectionately.

"Don't go to pieces, Dick."

Courtney ignored him and spoke to Gordon.

"What do you think? Am I going to pieces?"

The boy studied him intently. His expression was solicitous and he spoke earnestly.

"Well, I'll tell you, Dick—er, Major——"

"Damn the major, go ahead."

"Well, the fact is, you look—worn out. You need a rest."

"Is that all?"

Gordon hesitated.

"Say it. I'm thick-skinned. I can guess what you're thinking."

In the thin light the youngster flushed and shifted nervously.

"I'd say you were drinking too damned much," he answered candidly.

Courtney laughed.

"I have been. You're right. I'll have to do something about it."

He nodded and started on.

"By the way, Doug, look in on me in a little while, will you? Some things we ought to——"

"I'll be with you in ten minutes, Dick."

"Righto."

He went on to the bar. He nodded moodily to the men who were gathered there. When he stood at his accustomed place he became aware of their amused smiles at his dressing gown.

"Did something wake you up, Major?" inquired Bathurst mildly.

Courtney observed him with grim humor. His external irony covered his inner emotions as the old robe cloaked his body. He was hard and callous again, with something metallic and inhuman in his manner.

"Yes," he replied curtly, "ghosts. A whole squadron of them."

He laughed so brutally that men turned their eyes away and suddenly found themselves strangely shocked. But Bathurst alone understood. He nodded and his own chuckle was mellow.

"I hope," he said quietly, "there were a few G.H.Q. officers among them."

Courtney drained a tumbler of whisky and poured another. He did not speak again, and when he had drunk three he nodded silently to the group and left them. Bathurst shook his head.

"God," he said, in a subdued voice, "if he'd only take a little water with it."

The men about him laughed hollowly.

CHAPTER X

In the fleeting interlude before dawn an intangible destiny set the stage for one of its not infrequent miracles. Courtney, when he left the bar, went to his quarters prepared to plan the maneuvers of the double flight. Instead, he was interrupted by Douglas Scott. He saw at once that his visitor was ill at ease and harried. His own manner was one of detached interest.

"Pour yourself a spot, Doug." He indicated the extra chair beside the table, the liquor and glasses on a tray.

Scott helped himself to a liberal drink. Courtney half expected his sudden outburst.

"Dick, you've got to understand," he began and turned his steady gaze directly into Courtney's. "I—there's something I've been wanting to tell you ever since I found you here. You see, I——"

Courtney nodded slowly.

"Take your time, old fellow. You've been here only a few days."

Scott gestured impatiently.

"When I met you here," he resumed, "I saw

that you were—well, on edge. You'll have to admit, Dick, you've not been clean sober very much.''

"Granted." Courtney smiled.

"We've been so damned busy there hasn't been much time for straight talk. But before we take off this morning, I want to have it out, Dick.''

Courtney decided to make it easier for him. His voice was strangely controlled and he continued to smile with only a trace of weariness in his expression.

"I think I know what you're getting at, Doug. It's all right. There's nothing to explain.''

Scott leaned toward him.

"Then you saw the picture?''

"Yes.''

Scott flushed.

"I feel as though you think I'm a rotter, Dick. The fact is, I've been wanting to explain things. Sorry I didn't now, before you found out for yourself. But I wanted to avoid a row —you've been in a hellish mood. I wanted to talk it out with you—when we were both cold sober—and ourselves.''

Courtney bowed his head, so that his face was shadowed.

"What's the difference, old man? It was all

off between Lady Mary and me long ago. I
wish you happiness." He met Scott's gaze
levelly across the table.

"Then you do understand? You believe me,
Dick, when I say that I intended to tell you the
whole thing——"

"Of course. Why not?"

Scott studied his face penetratingly. He
found nothing there of doubt, or resentment
either. Only that heavy weariness which made
itself as apparent in the drawn face as it did
in Courtney's voice.

"I met her," Scott said, "when you were
doing scout patrol last spring. We heard you
were up at Arras then . . . it was in May."

Courtney nodded gravely.

"Yes. We had them on the run then."

He made a gesture with his hand, as if to dismiss it.

"You needn't explain, Doug. You don't owe
it to me, y'know."

"Yes, damn it, I do, Dick. If you'll listen."

He told how he met Lady Mary in a London
hospital. For a week he never knew that she
had broken off with Courtney. Then they kept
drifting together. He met her everywhere,
sometimes by accident, more often by design.
He ceased abruptly.

"Do you—do you still care for her, Dick?"

Courtney laughed so gently that his lie was a brilliant success.

"No. I have the highest regard for her, Doug. That is all. It's been off between Lady Mary and me for—years now."

He filled Scott's glass and his own and rose. "Good luck."

"Thanks, Dick. You're awfully fine."

Their glasses touched. Courtney set his down and pointed to the map that was spread on the table.

"I wanted to see you about this business." He sat down and lit a cigarette. "I'm going to disregard orders, Doug."

Scott stared across at him doubtfully.

"I mean," Courtney resumed in a matter-of-fact tone, "that if you agree to it, I'm not going to send these replacements out on this patrol."

Scott's face lighted.

"God, I'm glad. They wouldn't have a show."

"It means you'll have broken formation," Courtney went on. "I fancy I'll catch hell, but—" he shrugged. "I'll lie, damn it. I'll say we didn't have the crates in order—or something of the kind."

"That isn't a lie, it's fact," Scott put in

quickly. "We haven't got a ship in the lot that's fit to fight."

Courtney bent over the map.

"There'll be eleven of you then. Here's the layout."

He began to depict the territory in minute detail. He described certain objectives behind the enemy lines and pointed out ammunition dumps, railheads, bridges. Scott glanced up at him curiously.

"Where does all this stuff come from, Dick?"

"Confidential stuff from G.H.Q."

Scott idly picked up a sheet of paper on which were a mass of unintelligible letters and numerals. He stared at it.

"What the hell is this?"

Courtney smiled patiently.

"Code."

"You mean you can read it?"

"Yes."

"Good lord, what a job you fell heir to."

"Quite so."

They had still a little time before the dawn.

"Turn in, Doug. Tell Gordon he doesn't go."

Scott suddenly gripped his hand. He spoke impulsively.

"Thanks, fellow. You don't know how awfully much I——"

"Stow it," Courtney's voice was brittle again. "I'm only saving them for something later."

Alone again, he flung himself on the cot, clothed as he was, and surrendered to sleep. It was a deep stupor of exhaustion, untroubled by vague dreams. He awakened dully, unrelieved and more haggard than he had been before. But he had kept Lady Mary from his mind.

When the flight ships lay on the line and the old familiar banter flung back and forth from man to man, Courtney stood apart moodily silent. He glanced at each ship and wondered idly which of them would not return. The replacements were standing off watching the preparations with mingled disappointment and eager interest, curious for every detail.

He studied the sky. There would be fair visibility. He glanced at his watch and moved over to Scott's Bristol. He went up on the step and spoke curtly to the hooded pilot.

"Keep high over our lines, Doug. They might miscount, y'know. It'd save explanations."

Scott grinned and dropped his hand over on Courtney's shoulder.

"Count on me, Dick."

"Good luck."

He dropped down and stepped back to the line. As he bent his head over the watch again his right arm came up in signal. The mechanics spun the propellers all along the line and sprang away. Eleven motors coughed hollowly, then droned as the power took hold. In the next moment they were off, with Scott's plane running out ahead, its streamers fluttering in the wind.

Courtney stood watching them until his straining eyes could no longer discern the irregular formation against the distant eastern horizon. He wheeled sharply and without a word to the men about him moved toward the office. There he closeted himself, excluding even Bathurst, while he prepared for the worst that might happen.

He was steeled for anything except the miracle that occurred . . . it was that eleven ships came back.

He heard their rhythmic song while he was pouring over new code instructions from G.H.Q. He abandoned that instantly to go out to the field. Exultantly he counted the flight as it circled home.

He was waiting when Scott jumped lightly to the ground.

"All home, skipper," Scott shouted delightedly.

It seemed unbelievable. Courtney studied each ship as it ran into the line and paused for a word with each pilot. He saw the telltale holes in wings and fuselage, spots where the fabric fluttered in the late morning breeze, but every man was safe. He turned to Scott, a little bewildered.

"It's the first time that has happened since I came up here," he said. "God, Doug, perhaps our luck is changing."

He led them to the mess room, where he heard their swift accounts of the flight.

"It just happened," Scott told him confidentially. "We only ran into two flights . . . one of them on the way home. They didn't want to chase us too far over our lines, so they quit."

Courtney studied him.

"How many did you account for, Doug?"

"We got three, I believe. I'd like to verify them for the boys—y'know how they eat credit up at first?"

They smiled grimly. The talk ran on with the drinking. The drone of a diving motor halted the conversation all along the bar and at the tables. Courtney ran to the door and looked out. A Bristol was streaking down with the engine on full. Abruptly the power was throttled and the plane zoomed in a graceful curve. It leveled off again and pointed for the drome at a mild oblique.

Courtney turned savagely to Bathurst.

"Send that fellow to my office."

Bathurst smiled mysteriously and nodded.

"Very well, Major."

Directly Bathurst returned. His smile was enigmatic. He reported to Courtney.

"It was young Scott, sir—trying out Nine-O-Nine."

Courtney was aware that Douglas, standing beside him, stiffened. He turned to face him.

"I'm going to tear the pants right off him, Doug. Damn it, he'd no right to take that ship——"

"Go easy, old man. Y'know how a kid is."

"Easy hell. There's going to be discipline around here, or——"

Scott was grinning. Suddenly Courtney laughed and turned to the door.

"If you let on to Gordon that I'm not serious," he promised, "I'll ground both of you."

But his smile died as he strode to the office. When he entered the room he was grim and his voice was harsh.

"Did you take a ship up without permission, Gordon?"

The boy stood rigidly at attention.

"I'm sorry, sir. I did."

"Where did you go?"

"I flew up the line, sir, about twenty kilometers."

"Our own lines?"

Gordon flushed.

"Part way, Major."

"What did you see on the other side?"

"An Archie cut loose on me, sir, so I——"

"Went down after him, eh?"

"Yes, sir."

"What happened?"

He hesitated and swallowed.

"Well, something went wrong with the
damned controls—beg pardon, sir. But I
couldn't flatten off. I was working on the rudder, so I couldn't use the Lewis."

His face was becoming a deeper crimson in
his embarrassment.

"The Heinies must have thought I was diving to ram them, or something, because they
quit the gun mount and ran."

Courtney stood watching him severely. His
silence served to increase the boy's agitation.

"I got the flippers working and pulled out.
That gave me a chance to nose down again, sir,
so I did . . . and it put the Archie out of
business."

"Is that all?"

"Just about, Major."

"What else?"

"Well, a Fokker ran up after me. I tried to get away, sir, but he was too fast. So I cut straight back and he hung on. When we got over our lines I zoomed."

Scott coughed and went on haltingly.

"It must have surprised him, because he banked and got right under me. I couldn't miss him . . . he went down somewhere behind our lines, sir."

Courtney nodded curtly.

"Go to your quarters, Scott. I'm going to ground you ten days, I think. You're guilty of rotten insubordination. Didn't you understand the orders about solo flying?"

"Well, sir, y'see, when I first went up, I didn't intend to go away from the drome. But once I got up, I——"

Courtney gestured abruptly toward the door.

"You couldn't obey orders. Well, get to your quarters and think it over. You've got to get off on the right foot here, Scott."

He turned cold eyes on the boy's burning face and was stonily silent as he saw the smooth young jaws tighten and relax. Scott saluted, executed a proper about turn and marched from the room. Courtney slowly shook his head.

"What a lying hypocrite I have to be," he muttered.

Nevertheless, when G.H.Q. telephoned within an hour to report an enemy plane down behind Briey he lied yet again.

"Thank you," he replied curtly. "That verifies my report here for Lieutenant Scott—Gordon Scott . . . yes . . . I sent him over to put a damned Archie out of the way . . . yes, he did . . . and got the Fokker on the way home . . . all right . . . thanks."

He chuckled as he hung up the receiver. It was only the exceptional replacement who won a citation before his first patrol, he reflected. He hurried back to the bar to carry the news to Douglas. . . .

* * * * * * *

Unfortunately, the incident did nothing to make life easier. There was, of course, the momentary joy for Douglas and the ecstasy for Gordon. But even friends misunderstand. In point of fact, Courtney reminded himself again and again as the days passed that friends were less likely to understand than disinterested strangers, or even open enemies.

The word got around, of course, that he had winked at young Scott's disregard for the squadron regulations. Douglas himself, eager to spread his praise for Courtney, told far and

wide how the skipper had lied like a gentleman
and a soldier to save the boy.

It had the effect of adding to the C.O.'s popu-
larity, but it hurt discipline. By a succession
of those tricks of destiny which men learned to
accept, Douglas and Gordon Scott had come
through unscathed. But the Thirty-first Squadron had been battered. There were new names
on the blackboard now, when Courtney paused
to study them. Most of the old ones had been
erased with the soiled rag.

Still he found it almost impossible to enforce
an iron discipline. His own reputation came
back to flaunt him each time he called a smiling
young pilot before him. He had himself sown
the seeds of reckless insubordination that now
kept his nerves more than ever tingling.

So it was, as the days passed, that Courtney
discovered himself in the position that Brand
had held, which he had scorned so bitterly when
he first came up to Allonville. It was the
strange cycle of fate that pinned him helplessly,
as Brand had been in those first days of February. The strain of responsibility had taken
its toll.

He sat at his desk pawing through a maze
of documents. The whisky bottle that stood
always within his reach was half empty. The
desk was in confusion, no less than it had been

when Brand sat there. The room was filthy
again, too. He had fallen into the habit of
sleeping there, when the exertion of going to
his quarters seemed not worth the while. The
stale odor of liquor and tobacco hung heavily
on the air.

Bathurst looked in on him inquiringly. As
he glanced about the room the adjutant turned
an appealing gaze on Courtney.

"Major, why don't you take the château?
Brand meant that you should. You could rest
there—between times." He smiled wanly.

It was not the first time Bathurst had made
the suggestion. Courtney raised his bloodshot
eyes from the papers.

"Don't be an ass, Bathurst. You know damn
well why I don't want that place."

The adjutant shrugged.

"You could send her away, Major. Send her
back to Brand."

Courtney laughed. The humor of the idea
rather appealed to him. It would be droll, he
thought, to pack Celeste Lyons, bag and baggage, up to Brand at his new command. But
he dismissed the thought.

"Let her have the place," he said. "I'm all
right here."

He had frequently thought of going up to the
château. To himself he admitted the appeal

of Celeste, but invariably he gave up the idea.
Physical appeal was not enough. He could not
permit himself to become more of a beast than
he was, he thought. To take over Brand's work
was bad enough . . . to drink as he had done
. . . and to curse and exist here in the squalid
filth. But to take over his light o' love . . . not
that . . . not by a damned sight.

He looked up again at Bathurst.

"What's wrong with this?" he demanded.
"Isn't it good enough for a butcher? What the
hell should I do . . . spray it with perfume, or
burn incense?"

Bathurst grunted.

"A combination wouldn't do it any harm,
sir."

Courtney poured half a tumbler of whisky.
He drained it and sat back waiting for the hot
feel of it when the liquor seared his stomach.
He had drunk once for the mere social pleasure
it brought; later for the effect; but now he took
it for taste and effect. His palate had become
so hardened that ordinary food was tasteless.

He craved the seasoning of peppers and his
appetite cried out for sweets, rich chocolate and
sugared dainties that were as impossible here
as pâté de foie gras. But the craving ceased
when he drank. Then he wanted neither food,
nor water, nor sleep. Whisky and cigarettes,

with frequent black coffee, now and then a strip of red meat—these sufficed.

He was thinking all this while Bathurst stood watching him. The adjutant turned silently and went out. Courtney was scarcely aware of his departure, forgetful that he had been there.

They said he was drinking himself to death. By "they," he meant the squadron, the whole Thirty-first. As a matter of fact, it was said everywhere in the Royal Air Force, and Courtney knew it. He shrugged. To hell with them. They didn't understand that he wanted to kill every cell in his brain except those which functioned with this front.

He thought of his brain as a bit of sponge. One section of it governed his appetites. He had managed to kill off the cells that were concerned with food . . . and women . . . he wanted to nurse the drinking cells along. Then, he carried on with his crazy rambling thoughts, there must have been a part of the sponge that once held out for beauty and justice, calm thinking and spiritual things.

His guttural laugh sounded strange.

That part was done with. Now, if he could manage to keep a spark of life where the fighting cells were, let the world call him crazy. There were, he told himself grimly, just two functions left for him. One was to kill and the

A First National Picture.

The Dawn Patrol.

"BUCK UP OLD MAN, THERE'S ALWAYS THE CHANCE WE MAY ALL GET BACK."

other was to drink. Somehow, he would have to chloroform a part of the sponge that contained pity and kindness. They didn't belong.

Crazy or not, he reminded himself, this brain of his was clear on these code messages from headquarters. He had a vivid picture of the German offensive that was moving down upon Verdun with the slow certain pressure of a glacier. Already the gray hordes were rumbling by Abaucourt. From there the lines ran steeply south toward St. Mihiel.

The big push was coming. It would mean the finish of the Thirty-first. He poured another drink and shrugged as he swallowed it. These boys out beyond . . . Scott and the kid . . . Dunleavey and Fielding, all the rest of them . . . they were living and laughing and fighting with the silly hope that luck would bring them through.

Courtney laughed drunkenly. It sounded hollow and mocking.

"Luck," he snarled.

He recalled his own young belief in fortune, his own faith in the qualities of a friendly fate. But luck could not enter into it now . . . here were the first warning notes of demands that were inevitable. He knew in advance what the orders would be. . . .

Every man and every ship would be called.

England and France would let them all die
rather than move back an inch. He bent over
the map with its red line that showed the
front. Beside the map a code message gave
him the key to the enigma that would soon be
solved.

He was interpreting the code painstakingly
when Douglas Scott came in. At the threshold
he paused, observing Courtney with troubled
eyes.

"Good God, man, you look like a corpse."

Courtney repeated his brutal laugh.

"Deceptive, though, Doug. My chances to be
alive this time to-morrow are just a hundred to
one better than yours."

Scott considered this with a wry grimace.
He refused to take it seriously.

"You're an old black crow, Dick . . . caw-
ing over my grave."

Courtney pushed the bottle toward him.

"At least," he said, "that's a harmonious
picture. I'd hate to be a damned canary war-
bling over a grave—as though it was something to sing about."

Scott poured a small drink, limiting himself.

"Does it look so bad?" he asked.

Courtney shrugged.

"They're picking us to pieces bit by bit,
Doug . . . day by day. . . ."

"Yes."

"Well, when the Thirty-first goes up in formation . . . in the big finale, y'know . . . what'll they do then?"

Scott swallowed his drink, replaced the glass quietly and smiled.

"Curtain," he said.

"Curtain," Courtney repeated dully.

CHAPTER XI

THE finale was not far distant. It was as if an omnipotent stage director moved the puppets in his preparations for the inevitable last act. The guarded messages that came to Courtney by special courier were eloquent in their brevity. They were, of course, confidential. He was forced to keep his knowledge, even when he longed to explain himself.

In place of his former recklessness there had come into his manner a strange secretive quality that intensified his outward brutality. Scott ceased to drop in at his quarters, hurt by his savage replies to questions that had seemed to him harmless. Even Bathurst grew tight-lipped and quietly respectful.

The replacements spoke of him resentfully behind his back and stood in tense silence when he was present. Courtney spoke only when it was necessary, and then in the clipped tones of a man who is close to the outer edge of human decency. He no longer showed a spark of regret when the patrols reeled home with gaps in the formation, but only bitter anger at the loss of power. He had steeled himself so that emotion seemed to have died in him. Even his anger was controlled, like a buried torrent in the rock beneath an impregnable mountain.

Bathurst, more familiar with the situation than the others, tried to explain it to a group in the bar.

"The skipper can't last under the strain," he shook his head slowly and there was a positive sound in his words. "He's got to break, sooner or later."

Douglas Scott took him up scornfully.

"That's a lot of bally rot, Bathurst. There's no call for his damned ugliness. We're not the only squadron that's catching hell. He's not the only C.O. who's in a tight seat. Damn it, Dick could be human."

Bathurst observed him patiently.

"Quite true, old man. But as it happens, there isn't another Courtney, either. It takes a phlegmatic man for that job, Doug. Dick is a flyer—not a brass hat." He sipped his wine, and when he spoke again there was infinite understanding in his tone.

"Y'know, Doug," he drawled now and his eyes were thoughtful, "the chaps who are running this war are so expert that they take everything into consideration—like God, y'know —even the tiniest sparrow—but there's one thing they overlook. And it's more important than everything else.''

He finished his drink. The others were silent.

"That's the little matter of human nature," he added. "They mark down machines in one row and men in another." His smile was a little sad, and his eyes. "They get ammunition and horse power and human guts all mixed up together, fellows. If they didn't, Dick Courtney would have a roving commission."

There was a momentary silence.

"I see what you mean," Scott said. "In a way, you're right too, Bathurst. But I still contend that it isn't necessary for Dick to go to pieces. Why damn it, he's worse than Brand. Didn't he threaten to ground me for ten days for a solo? And let a new kid lead A Flight! He's been helling around the front since the start. He ought to understand better than anyone else."

Bathurst smiled.

"He does," he said.

But when he returned to the office after his attempt to justify Courtney, he told himself that he had failed. It would have to be something more potent than words, some cataclysmic incident in tune with the life of the man him-

self. Courtney, he thought, could be explained
only in deeds. Words somehow failed to regis-
ter in the storm of his existence.

As he entered the outer office he heard
Courtney's voice.

"There will be no reinforcements, you say?"
The tone was ominously controlled.

Courtney was replacing the telephone when
Bathurst walked in. He nodded and Bathurst
caught some swift significance in his silence.
Courtney brushed the hair back from his temples. His hand was trembling, but there was
nothing new about that. He had come to the
place now where his whole body twitched convulsively, so that he had no control over it.
When he took a drink it would cease for a time.
He looked up at the adjutant.

"Before the week is out, Bathurst—*finis* for
the Thirty-first."

Bathurst forced a smile.

"There isn't any end to anything, Dick—it
goes on and on."

Courtney filled his glass and drained it. He
felt better immediately and color came to his
grayish cheeks. He, too, found it possible to
smile.

"Nevertheless," he said, with conviction,
"the end. The big push is on Friday. G.H.Q.

just verified it. We're to throw every man in
the air—starting now—including replacements.''

"Good God!"

"Yes," the inflection was sardonic, "quite
so. Four patrols a day—strafing infantry—
guarding river crossings—the usual rot. I'll
have written verification with detailed instructions sometime to-day.''

Bathurst sank into a chair.

"Then it's the real thing. That's—that's
bad," he muttered.

Courtney's laugh was staccato.

"Bad," he repeated, "for us. We'll be under everything that flies—cold meat for Von
Richter.''

A hesitant knock sounded on the door. Courtney barked:

"Well?"

Sergeant Bott jerked the door open and reported: "The replacements are quartered, sir.''

"All right. Send the gang to the mess
room.''

"Very well, sir.''

Courtney turned to Bathurst. "Get the field
sergeant out—all ships ready for patrol.''

"Right away?"

"Now.'' The word snapped like an oath.

Courtney assembled the papers on his desk in

a heap and chose a blank detail sheet to take with him to the mess room. He paused for another drink. When he had taken it he rubbed his jowls that were bristling with dark beard and grinned.

"What the hell's the difference?" he muttered.

His white soft shirt was open at the throat and his uniform was wrinkled from having slept in it. He happened to glance up at his leather harness that suspended from a peg in the wall. His automatic glinted dully beneath the dust.

He remembered the last time he had fired it. The surprised Heinie stiffening in his cockpit— the whirling black plane. He laughed and it sounded like a growl. He wondered why he had never thought of that gun before while he sat in this room like a prisoner. It offered the way out. . . .

Oddly, he laughed again, and this time there was humor in the sound. He answered his own question inwardly. He had not thought of the automatic because the thing was unthinkable. Whatever else he might do, he would never quit. They couldn't force him to that.

He found the squadron assembled in the mess room. A silence fell over them. He nodded without speaking directly to anyone. He went to his favorite place at the end of the bar me-

chanically and, leaning on his elbows, with his
back against the counter, faced the group. They
were watching him expectantly.

"Gentlemen, I'm able to share one of G.H.Q.'s
little secrets with you—we go to work immediately."

His ironic gaze swept the half-circle of faces.
Most of them were boyish faces, rounded and
smooth.

"Fritz is starting the big push day after to-
morrow," he went on quietly. "They're starting minor advances now—strategic points—
river crossings—that sort of thing."

His voice was so controlled that it puzzled
them. He might have been recounting some
insignificant bit of news that had drifted back
from the line.

"We do four patrols a day, commencing in
the morning. It means every man up."

An excited youngster could not contain himself.

"Gad, now we'll see something!"

Courtney nodded casually.

"You'll patrol the third sector, opposite the
Sixth army."

He paused to light a cigarette.

"It means," he resumed, "that you'll have
the dirty work. Low flying, y'know—keep
snapping at the Fritz infantry—strafe their

supply trucks. They'll try to bring up shock troops, of course. You'll have to worry them."

Douglas Scott had moved up into the first row of those who listened to the impassive voice that seemed to drone without inflection or feeling.

"You're up against Von Richter," Courtney added. "You know that, anyway. He'll have flights over you, I fancy."

He shrugged.

"It won't be pretty." His face was expressionless, like weather-beaten stone. It was peculiarly in accord with the flat metallic sound of his voice.

"I've ordered inspection of all ships. I wish you luck, gentlemen."

He turned abruptly to the bar and reached for the bottle which Crandall had set out for him in anticipation. There was a sudden burst of eager talk, mingling with laughter and a good deal of horseplay that came with the release of suppressed emotions. Douglas Scott caught his brother's arm and drew him up beside Courtney.

"You didn't mean these youngsters are in this, did you, Dick?" It was evident that he was restraining himself.

"Every man we've got, Doug."

Scott braced himself and his eyes blazed.

"These boys—against Von Richter——"

For one instant Courtney's manner changed. His voice sounded pleadingly: "Hold on, Doug, old man, I——"

"Hold on, hell! If you think I'm going to lead these kids against that show you're crazy. Why, damn it, they don't know what they're up against. They haven't a chance."

The spell was broken. Courtney's momentary lapse into humanness had come and gone. The kindness vanished from his face and he gazed at Scott with hard expressionless eyes. Gordon stepped between them, facing his his brother.

"Doug, you——"

Scott whirled on him.

"Shut your mouth." He turned instantly to Courtney: "I won't take them."

The men about them stood awkwardly, uncertain what they should do or say. Courtney did not raise his voice.

"I said every man up."

Scott's lips curled in a sneer.

"Yes—you did, Courtney. You, who used to talk about schoolboys in canvas coffins."

Courtney straightened and his jaws moved convulsively.

"Get the hell out. Prepare your flight."

They stood tensely, their eyes level and hard. Scott was first to lower his gaze.

"All right," he said quietly. "I think I can understand—why you'd like me out of the way. But Gordon—these kids——"

The gray pallor that lay upon Courtney's face turned a darker shade. He gulped and his hands clenched at his sides. His voice came huskily.

"You don't—mean that. Get going, Scott—before I—forget myself."

He turned his back on the man who had been his friend. In the electric silence the breathing of the group there was distinct. Behind the little bar Crandall moved uncertainly and a bottle rang loudly against its mate. There was a sudden shuffling of feet on the plank floor, subdued voices and a nervous, muffled laugh. Courtney was alone except for Crandall. He poured a full glass of liquor and raised it mockingly.

"To the Thirty-first, Crandall."

The little man behind the bar hastily poured a thimbleful of whisky into a tumbler. He forced a wan smile.

"Here's to it, sir."

When he returned to the office Courtney sent Bathurst for Gordon Scott. The boy came in hastily. He halted and drew himself up to attention.

"Come in, Gordon. Sit down."

Courtney motioned him to a chair.

"I'm sorry, Gordon, that I——"

The boy half rose.

"Dick," he cried out, "don't talk that way. For God's sake, it's you I'm sorry for. Doug was an ass. I don't want you to worry, Dick. I can hold my own——"

His pent-up emotion released itself in a burst as he sprang up and leaned over the desk.

Courtney smiled.

"No. Doug was right. You might as well get it straight now, Gordon. You can fly, yes. But you haven't had the experience for combat —of this sort. You fellows up from school haven't had the chance."

"But, Dick, I've been——"

"You've been up in a dog fight or two," the interruption was gentle. "This time, Gordon, you're stacking against the best men and ships in the air. I want you to know——"

Scott's head drooped, but he raised it swiftly to turn confident eyes upon Courtney.

"Suppose you're right, Dick. What of it? I'll get somebody—before I go."

"Righto. If you can take it in that spirit, Gordon, you'll be all right. Just try to keep your head. There's many a time when you can nurse a ship down on a long glide."

"Center the controls in a spin." The voice was eager, full of young confidence. "I've done it, Dick—flattened off first rate."

Courtney studied him curiously. He wondered if he was doing the right thing to talk straight out to the boy. It could have the effect of stretching his nerves until they snapped, or, if he was made of the right stuff, perhaps it would save him. He decided to follow through.

"There's been a sort of tradition in the Thirty-first," he went on, thoughtfully. "I know you new chaps will carry on with it. I wish you'd mention it to the others, Gordon, if you have a chance."

"Of course."

Courtney hesitated for words. Presently, he spoke and he was strangely gentle. The hard lines in his face had relaxed and his eyes were kind.

"When it comes to the very worst," he said quietly; "that is, when a fellow knows that he's done for—when there isn't another chance, y'understand——"

"Yes?"

"Well, the thing to do, if it can possibly be managed, Gordon, is to ram the nearest enemy ship. Lock with him—put him out of it—go down together.''

Scott's eyes had widened as he listened and his muscles tensed. At the grating sound of that last—go down together—he nodded abruptly. The tension left him and he laughed.

"I've always thought that would be the way," he said quietly. "Count on me, Dick."

Courtney reached out, and their hands met in a swift touch of understanding.

"Good enough, Gordon, old man. Good luck."

As he went out the boy's eyes were gleaming with resolve. His square young shoulders were set and he held his head up proudly. He had been accepted on an equal basis at last. He would never again be a boy. Something grim and strong and very wonderful had come into his life. He told himself in that high moment that death held no fear. Courtney's words had vanquished it. Courtney, he thought, was very splendid. He would always remember him like that.

But Courtney, lingering at his desk, suddenly lowered his head into the circle of his arms. Something choked in his throat and he could not sob. His eyes burned hideously, but he could not weep. He had mastered his emotions until they no longer fought against him.

He sat up directly and, resting his chin in his hand, stared unseeingly into the shadows of the room. His mind still recoiled at that last thrust from Scott. It could not be possible that Doug actually believed what he had said. He began to question himself in a relentless analysis.

The answers sprang back in his mind so swiftly, with so little time for reasoning, that he smiled. Not even Lady Mary Cambridge would believe that he wished to sacrifice Doug Scott. But he could understand Doug's flood of uncontrollable anger—the unreasoning, unreasonable rage that swept him when he knew that Gordon was doomed.

Courtney opened a drawer of his desk and drew out a leather-bound book. It was one of those which he had brought from home to read in the occasional moments of his leisure. He would mark a place for Doug and leave the book where he would find it. He opened the book and found the quotation readily. Oddly, and he smiled again as the thought recurred to him, it was the work of an enemy—Friedrich Nietzsche's *Thus Spake Zarathustra*. . . .

"We like neither to be spared by our best enemies, nor by those whom we love from our heart of heart. Let me tell you the truth!"

He underscored that with the red pencil that

he used for marking his flight charts. He
read on:

"My brethren in war! I love you from my
heart's heart. I am and was your like. And,
besides, I am your best enemy. Therefore let
me tell you the truth!

The red pencil struck swiftly as fragmentary
lines found a chord in his own mind. . . .
"War and courage have done more great things
than charity. . . . Not your pity, but your
bravery, hath hitherto saved those who had met
with an accident . . . they call you heartless;
but your heart is genuine, and I love the shame
of your heartiness. . . ."

Courtney turned a page. "Rebellion, that is
superiority in the slave. Let your superiority
be obedience . . . what is long life worth!
What warrior wisheth to be spared!"

He paused with his finger touching the spot
over the little book, absorbed. Page after page
he read and frequently paused to draw a thin
red line beneath a passage. Strange, he thought
how some of them struck home. . . .

"One day thou wilt see no longer what is
high for thee, and much too close what is low
for thee."

The high road and the low road again . . .
the high soul and the low. . . .

He marked still one more line and this one he

underscored doubly . . . "To do great things
is hard; but to command great things is still
harder."

He closed the book and thrust it back into
the drawer. On second thought he brought it
out again and wrote swiftly on the flyleaf . . .
"To Doug, with whom my credit account is in
the red—Dick." Then he dropped the book in
its place and began to study the map with its
fantastic hieroglyphics that were sacred to
G. H. Q.

There lay the secret of the next few days.
Printed names of towns and villages that fell
upon the ear like a melody, Ste. Cecile and
Carignan, Arracourt and Provenchere . . . the
wide sweep of the Western Front from Belgium
to Switzerland.

He paused with his finger touching the spot
which would be the third sector and across from
it the German Sixth Army. His eyes acquired
a puzzled expression, as he gazed curiously at
the tip of his finger. He thought: where my
finger is now some of these youngsters will go
down. Scott, probably, and with him Gordon.

Doug will damn me with his last breath . . .
call me a kid butcher . . . he will think I sent
him up so that . . .

He jerked his finger from the map and
straightened in his chair.

"Hell," he growled aloud, "I'm letting my nerves slip. Got to tighten up."

He reached for the whisky bottle and laughed in his throat.

"Down with it—have to kill that part of the sponge."

Outside the mechanics were testing planes. The day was drawing to a close and another dawn was not far off. If he lived until the finish, Courtney mused, he would never get up again until long after sunrise. He would never read a poem that told of dawn. He would never hear the word without a shudder. It would forever have the ring of death in its sound and he would associate it always with the word that invariably was part of it here—the dawn patrol.

He stood up uncertainly and gazed at Brand's moon-faced clock. The hands pointed to quarter after four. Suddenly Courtney cried out and smothered the sound. His eyes blazed. In just twelve hours the flights would be taking off. . . .

He seized the bottle from his desk and flung it at the clock. His frenzied aim was accurate. The round white face vanished in a burst of flying glass and brown liquor.

The crash brought Bathurst on the run. He found Courtney standing in the center of the

floor staring down at the clock and laughing
hysterically.

"Look at it, Bathurst. Look, damn it, it's
still going. I knocked it all to hell, man—and
it's still going."

Bathurst took his arm and led him to the
door.

"Don't bother about it, Courtney, old man.
Get a little sleep now. Let me send some grub
up to your quarters."

Courtney stared at him. Slowly his eyes regained their sanity and he sagged. His head
bowed until it drooped and he spread his hands
at his sides in a gesture of resignation.

"Sorry, Bathurst. Something got the best of
me for a minute. I'm all right now, quite
all right——"

"Of course. A bit of food, skipper—some
sleep. You'll be fit as——"

Courtney raised his head and eyed him
steadily.

"Yes, fit as ever, of course."

He straightened abruptly as the door flung
open and Douglas Scott came in. He spoke
abruptly:

"Dick, I came in to apologize. I was a
cad——"

Courtney smiled and his voice was steady.

"Forget it, Doug. We all go to pieces. God knows it was your turn."

"But I said——"

Courtney shut him off with a gesture that did not escape Bathurst. He smiled and withdrew.

"Get a spot of grub, Major," he called from the door.

Courtney nodded and faced Douglas.

"Let it go, fellow. I didn't think you meant it. Let's drop it now."

Scott returned his gaze steadily.

"Gordon told me he had seen you. The kid understands—better than I did, Dick. Thanks. You're awfully white."

They went out together into the twilight. The rumble in the east was deeper and the sky was black and dull copper by turns.

"The fun is beginning," Courtney said.

"Yes. The lines must be catching hell about now."

They moved on toward the mess room. Scott turned his head to observe his companion's face.

"I feel like a dog, Dick."

"Drop it. Don't you suppose I understand? My own nerves aren't so sweet."

There was another brief silence.

"One thing, Dick," Scott insisted quietly. "I want you to know that it was my own rotten inferiority that made me fly off. Y'see fellow, I'm not fooling myself. I know you're the better man—and it doesn't seem fair."

Courtney shot his glowing cigarette to the ground.

"You talk like a schoolboy, Doug." He laughed and forced it to sound real. "I'd count on Mary's judgment any day. When she threw me over, she knew me. And when she picked you—she knew who was the better man. Anyway, it's silly to talk about it, Doug. The whole thing is done with and forgotten. Let's forget it, will you?"

Scott studied him carefully, but saw no deceit in his eyes. He nodded moodily, still unconvinced.

"All right, Dick. I won't talk about it any more."

CHAPTER XII

THE raucous gramophone in the mess room, the harsh unnatural laughter and the babble of voices all failed that night to crowd out the angry voices of the guns. Men spoke of the advance lightly and laughed, but their eyes were vaguely haunted. To Courtney the scene was stale. This high courage under pressure was becoming almost commonplace. He thought of a line he had read somewhere . . . "Courage has always been the best of fun, and so to end is but to have begun."

He drank steadily, but unlike the others, he talked little. He left them while they were still pretending. On the way to his quarters he stopped in at the office, where Bathurst was on lonely vigil for whatever word might come from G. H. Q.

"Well, they seem to be making a night of it," Bathurst moved his head in the direction of the intermittent rumble.

Courtney nodded.

"Call me if anything comes through, Bathurst."

"Of course, skipper. Sleep if you can. God knows you need it."

Courtney went in to his desk and found the leather-bound book. He took it to Scott's room, where he found Gordon staring from the darkness toward the strange red glow in the east. The boy was lying on his bunk. He sat up and recognized Courtney in the dim light from the door.

"Oh, come in, Dick. I thought it was Doug."

"Hello, Gordon. He'll be along directly. I just wanted to leave a book for him."

He dropped the little volume on a table.

"What is it, Dick?" Curiously.

"Nietzsche, the German."

"Oh, yes. We used to tackle that at school— *Thus Spake Zarathustra*—written in the biblical style."

"Did you like it?"

Gordon laughed softly.

"Some of it. He had an interesting philosophy. I didn't understand much of it, but he wrote like a good egg."

"Yes, I think he believed in happiness . . . but I believe in sleep, too. Get under the blanket, Gordon. Don't think about it—just try to fancy you're home."

The boy drew the cover about his shoulders and smiled into the gloom. His eyes, when he

looked up, were full of dread that he tried
to conceal.

"Good idea, Dick, old fellow. I'll try it. It
ought to be easy that way."

Courtney lingered a moment, then turned
abruptly and left him with no further word.
He could not trust himself to talk. He went
to his quarters and this night, instead of the
usual ritual over the waiting bottle, he delved
immediately into his trunk to draw out the
portrait of Lady Mary. He held it before him
for a moment and smiled.

With a penknife he slit the cardboard that
backed the frame and the photograph fell out.
With it came the verse . . . "To every man
there openeth a Way, and Ways and a Way."

"I'll keep the verse, Mary," he spoke half
aloud.

He was still uncertain enough of his way, he
reflected, but at least one path was clear, even
though it was but a wandering little trail that
diverged from the great high road. He must
put her forever out of his life and his mind.
With that done, he told himself, he might yet
reclaim what remained of life. He would master himself.

His lean brown fingers tore at the heavy tex-
ture of the portrait gently, as if they hated their
task. Again and again he ripped the paper un-

til the table beneath his hands was heaped with
tiny fragments. He swept them into a paper
and, going to the stone doorsill, touched a match
to the lot. The flame sprang up hungrily and
painted high lights on his face. His body was
limned in the glow and the old rocks of the
building became rose-colored.

He leaned there against the doorframe until
the still glowing flakes rose on the breeze and
scattered. They were, he thought, like his
memories of Mary Cambridge . . . still exist-
ent, but forever lost . . . reduced to ashes in
a fierce flame, but not entirely obliterated. He
could see the little heap of gray that had been
the portrait. He touched it with his boot and a
soft wind completed the havoc.

His room, when he closed the door, seemed to
have vaguely changed. All the warmth was
gone from it and he had no desire for the
brandy that sparkled amber-tinted in the light.
Sleep was out of the question. There was still
work to be done. He shrugged into the leather jacket that he preferred to the tailored blouse
of his uniform.

When he returned to the office he ordered
Bathurst to bed and was savage when the adjutant protested. Alone in the foul little room
he began to plot a chart of the territory from
the code instructions of the intelligence division.

He worked mechanically, falling into the way of the headquarters staff unconsciously. He took into consideration the probable altitude of the various flights, the outlay of machines and ammunition, wind resistance and all of these factors which would enter into the action at dawn. But he had ceased entirely to consider the human equation. It was a victory over himself of which he was unaware.

It worked out quite simply on paper. The pursuit ships would go up to ten thousand feet, while the attack planes dived over the enemy lines so low that their pilots could see the faces of the men in the trenches. The low bombers would cross at three hundred feet and take the machine gun and rifle fire, while the day bombers hovered twelve thousand feet aloft with their heavy charges. He pictured the action and suddenly visioned Scott diving over the line.

All his grim mechanical indifference was swept away then and his temporary victory became a reversal. He reached unsteadily for the bottle and swore hideously when the liquor slopped over the top of his glass . . . but instead of drinking it, he poured it on the floor.

He was sitting there when Bathurst came in at half-past three. The bottle was empty, but Courtney was steady and self-possessed, more so, Bathurst thought, then he had been earlier in the night.

"Hello. Better route 'em all out, old man."

The adjutant laughed indulgently.

"Most of the crowd is in the bar, Dick."

"Better get the field sergeant out then. Have everything ready sharp. We're timed this morning."

When he was left alone again Courtney went to the window that faced to the east. Daylight already was beginning to dull the sullen glow that hung there. The rumble came though, irregular and vicious. He gazed steadily toward the streaked sky until his sight was dimmed. He turned back to the desk and his lips were drawn in a hard straight line. There could be no place for mercy now, he told himself. Even a semblance of it would be futile.

He went out to the tarmac and stood watching the mechanics as they hauled the ships out to the line. The pilots came out in groups and stood about him, forcing their subdued laughter, trying to be unconcerned.

Gordon Scott approached him.

"Mornin', Major."

"Hello, Gordon. Sleep all right?"

"Like a top."

"Good."

The boy hesitated and suddenly thrust out his hand.

"Well, we're off."

"Good luck, Gordon."

Scott left him and went to his plane. Douglas moved after him and Courtney could hear his voice.

"Take second position on my right."

"Righto, Doug."

It was only repetition for Courtney. The scene sickened him, but he remained stolidly emotionless, a tall dark shadow that was stationary among other moving shadows in the gradual dawn. The flight leaders waved with studied nonchalance and went up into the cockpits. Douglas Scott laughed down at Courtney, but his expression was a grimace, like a painted gray mask.

The contact cry leaped along the line from ship to ship and the propellers whirled. The thunder of the flight was like heavy firing. Scott's slender little plane flashed into the wind and pointed sharply upward. The rest of them followed it.

Beside Courtney, Bathurst slowly crumpled a match between his thumb and forefinger. As the flight lifted above the distant pines he tossed the pieces into the air and caught them.

"How many?" Courtney asked dully.

Bathurst examined the bits.

"Three."

"We won't get off so light."

With that Courtney turned abruptly and walked toward the office. Bathurst remained on the field, vaguely miserable, staring into the eastern sky that was showing streaks of lemon-yellow and orange. When he cupped one hand to his ear he could catch the diminishing drone of the flight, but they had passed beyond the range of his limited vision. Bathurst's private tragedy was an astigmatism that had kept him out of a plane.

But still, he often reminded himself, he had managed to observe considerable in spite of the bad eye.

*   *   *   *   *   *   *   *

When he went back to the office Bathurst found Courtney at his desk. He was sitting rigidly, facing forward and a fresh bottle, now partly empty, stood within easy reach.

"Ease off, skipper. There's nothing you can do about it."

Courtney gazed at him steadily as though he had not heard.

"If this were the finish," Bathurst rambled on soothingly, "you could worry like that and come through. But hell," he shrugged, "it's only the beginning. Another set will go out to-morrow and another——"

Courtney was listening attentively. He nodded.

"I was thinking exactly that," he said.

"So what's the use?" asked Bathurst.

For a time they were silent.

Courtney spoke flatly: "If it weren't Von Richter——"

"It would be some other hellion. After all, Major, a lot of Heinies used to talk about you just as you're talking about Von Richter. You weren't noted for your gentle qualities, y'know."

Courtney nodded. Bathurst's tone of mild humor strangely did not annoy him.

"They didn't come so young, though." His reply was peculiarly quiet, more as if he were speaking to himself. "It was man to man— no kids."

"Oh, hell." Bathurst made a gesture of disbelief. "You were just a kid yourself—all of them were."

Courtney stared at him without resentment.

"You don't understand, Bathurst. We were fairly young, yes, but we came into it early— grew up with it. Don't you see? We aged a hundred years in those two. These boys are tossed into it raw, don't you see?"

His question rose plaintively and he kept looking at Bathurst as though he wanted him to understand. He poured drinks and smoked incessantly while he kept looking toward the east window. Dawn brightened into brilliant day and its beauty was oddly undisturbed by the constant roaring of the guns. In the pines of Allonville forest the first birds of spring ignored the strangeness of their universe. Magpies sounded their raucous notes and high overhead some larks wheeled in the sun.

Courtney rose frequently and went to the door. When he held it open the aroma of breakfast cooking beyond the mess room floated in, and to Bathurst was appetizing. Courtney failed to smell it.

"How about a spot of coffee?" Bathurst approached him.

"No, thanks." Courtney smiled thinly. "I couldn't swallow."

Bathurst grinned.

"You could make the same motion in your throat as when you take that," he indicated the liquor.

But Courtney ignored the irony and stood gazing into the sky.

The flight had been out almost to the limit of its fuel when at last he heard the approaching drone. Bathurst had breakfasted and returned carrying a pot of coffee. It still stood untouched on the desk. Courtney moved jerkily and stared at him. They went together to the door. From narrowed eyes Courtney studied the sky. Beside him, Bathurst waited, not venturing to strain his optic nerves against the brilliance.

"Five," Courtney said flatly. "Your match was wrong."

"Five—gone?"

"Five."

The leader of the first circled above the airdrome once and dived with his power on.

"That's Scott—Doug." Courtney's voice was still toneless.

They stood motionless as the plane flattened off, the engine throttled, then sped to the ground. They saw Scott spring over the side and head toward them on a drunken lope. He came straight to the door. As he drew near they saw that his face was distorted. He plunged up before them and motioned toward the office.

The three of them stood inside the door. As yet no one had spoken. Scott broke the silence with stabbing ferocity.

"Well, Courtney—he went down—in flames— you butcher!"

For an instant Courtney staggered. He put

out one hand to steady himself against the door.

"Doug—old man——"

But Scott stepped in close. His eyes blazed insanely.

"That's over with, Courtney. From now on you're just a drunken rotter who ranks me. Do you understand that? You sent that kid up—you even told him—how to die."

His mouth opened and twisted in a snarl.

"You," his voice rose and trembled, "telling that boy—how to go out—while you sat here swilling liquor."

He whirled and ran from the room. Courtney stared at the blank expanse of the wooden door. His shoulders sagged a little and he turned wearily to his chair behind the desk. He sank down into it and suddenly lowered his head into the circle of his arms. He did not speak. The swift ferocity of Scott's venom had numbed him.

Bathurst walked over and touched his shoulder. Courtney did not move. Bathurst picked up the nearly empty bottle, poured the remaining liquor into his own glass and drank it. Then he went silently to the closet and brought out a fresh bottle. He set it on the desk and left the office.

In an hour he returned. For a few minutes he typed in his cubby outer office, then went in to Courtney. He pretended that he did not see the anguish in the lined face, nor did he apparently glance at the bottle now more than half empty. Courtney was lolling at his desk, no longer sober.

"Here's the flight report, skipper. Shall I call G.H.Q. or——"

Courtney waved the paper aside.

"To hell with 'em, Bathurst. To hell with 'em. Tell me—how did little Gordon Scott go out?"

"Twenty of Von Richter's ships got over them. The kid went down in flames."

"Fighting?"

Bathurst smiled tensely.

"He rammed a Fokker. They were still locked when they fell. Scott watched it."

"God!"

It was the first and only time that Bathurst was ever privileged to see his commanding officer break. For that particular reason it affected him intensely. When Courtney tried to rise and fell back into his chair, the adjutant sprang around the desk and seized his shoulders. Courtney was only semiconscious.

Without pausing to consider anything Bathurst lifted the heavy body in his arms and carried it as though he was only just aware of his strength. He walked with his burden to the outer door and two mechanics, seeing him, came up on the run.

"The major is ill," he told them curtly.

He saw the swift exchange of their eyes, and growled. Of course, they thought he was drunk, he told himself bitterly. He went on to Courtney's quarters and gently lowered the heavy body upon the cot. He covered it with a light blanket and started back to the office, intending to call the M.O.

*   *   *   *   *   *   *   *

Late in the afternoon Courtney awoke. No medical officer had come in answer to Bathurst's call, but, being ignorant of events, Courtney was not concerned. He sat up dizzily and grinned. His head ached horribly and his eyes were stabbing points. At first he attributed his condition to the usual cause, but as his brain cleared he remembered. He got up immediately and did not bother to shave, or refresh himself. He went across the road along the edge of the drome, bent and haggard, dragging his feet in the dirt as he stumbled.

He was oblivious of the callous smiles of field men who looked at him carelessly and shrugged. He lurched into the office upon the startled Bathurst.

"Good heavens, Major. You're on the sick list. What are you——"

"Be quiet, Bathurst. I'm quite all right. Heard from headquarters yet?"

"Yes, I reported in and also I told 'em you were flat."

"Damned silly of you. Now they'll check up on me—find me drunk on duty—all that rot."

"But the M.O. said he'd come, Dick."

"To hell with him. Won't see him. Tell him I'm quite all right."

Outside an army car drew up. Bathurst hurried out. He came face to face with Major Brand.

"Major! I say, it's jolly good to see you here again, sir."

"Hello, Bathurst. Glad to see you."

They shook hands. Brand was looking fit. He had lost weight and his face was smooth and his eyes clear. He smiled placidly.

"Where's Courtney?"

Bathurst turned a troubled gaze toward the interior office. Brand nodded quickly and walked in without being announced. He halted in the door. Courtney was standing at his desk pouring a drink. His hand trembled so that the liquor kept spilling. His eyes were bloodshot and shadowed. His hair was rumpled and untrimmed and his soiled shirt was open at the throat.

At the sight of Brand he straightened. A

slow smile spread over his lips and he chuckled drunkenly.

"Well, Major," he spoke huskily, "you certainly were right."

He evinced no surprise, no emotion whatever. Brand walked across the room and paused at the desk.

"Glad to see you, Courtney."

"Thanks. Have a drink."

"Yes, I will. Thank you."

His gaze traveled fleetingly about the room and his lips twitched.

"The place hasn't changed much."

"No."

Courtney gulped his liquor. Brand drank slowly.

"What brought you back to this hole, Brand?"

Brand put his glass down deliberately and took a chair. Courtney sagged heavily into his own.

"Headquarters sent me—they say you raise hell about orders."

Courtney remained silent.

"This business was too important to argue about, so they told me to come down in person."

Courtney nodded slowly. Brand leaned a little forward and his expression became grave. His voice was crisp.

"The intelligence lads brought word of this," he began. "It's been verified, so we're sure."

He paused to assemble his thoughts.

"You've had instructions about the push—but we've got a way to stop it, Courtney."

At that Courtney sat upright and his manner changed almost miraculously. He became alert, tight-lipped and his eyes fastened steadily on Brand.

"Their whole advance," the major resumed, "depends on their concentration at a munition dump—I've got the chart here. When that's out of the way—they're stopped."

Courtney nodded.

"The hell of it is," Brand continued, "this dump is sixty kilometers behind the lines."

Their eyes met squarely.

"A bombing squadron couldn't hope to get in that far. The whole German air force would be on their tails."

"Naturally."

Brand tapped the desk with his finger. "So you see, Major, it's a one-man job. That's what I'm here for. It's up to your squadron—the Thirty-first."

Courtney studied him quietly.

"You realize, of course, that it's a one-way flight. Even if our ships carried enough fuel—

a man couldn't get in that far and come out of it."

Brand bent his head gravely.

"Exactly," he said.

There was a silence that seemed to throb. Courtney leaned forward abruptly and his face came close to Brand's.

"I'll not send one of my men on that. It's suicide."

Brand gazed at him steadily.

"It has to be done, Courtney—at dusk this evening. I'm sorry." Finality was in his tone and manner.

Courtney leaned back in his chair and gazed at the liquor bottle. His face was strangely calm. A queer smile was playing at the corners of his mouth.

"Bathurst."

The adjutant appeared in the door.

"Assemble the men in the mess room."

"Very well, sir." The door swung to.

Brand watched curiously as Courtney rose.

"Calling for a volunteer?"

"Yes."

They found the mess room crowded. A swift silence came upon the group as they entered. There were a few hurried greetings for Brand. Courtney leaned against the bar and faced them.

He was like an unkempt vagabond in a room full of well-groomed, clean-faced youngsters. He explained Brand's mission in a flat monotone.

"Whoever goes won't get back," he concluded.

Before he could shift his position at the bar, Scott sprang before him.

"My job."

A dozen voices echoed his words.

"I was first." He stared at Courtney. "Do I get it?"

Courtney shrugged.

"It's yours. Thanks." He turned to Bathurst. "Have Scott's ship overhauled right away—load incendiary bombs."

Brand reached for Scott's hand.

"Good luck, youngster. There's a chance or two—keep a stiff upper lip."

Scott laughed. "There isn't—really," he said. "But I'll watch for 'em, Major."

Courtney took Brand back to his car. They paused.

Brand said, "I'm sorry, Dick."

Courtney answered him quietly, "Good-by."

"Good-by."

He stood watching the car as it circled rapidly among the pines and disappeared.

When he went back to the office, Bathurst was ahead of him.

"Tell Scott I want him. You can stay away. I want to see him alone."

Bathurst was a little hurt. Courtney smiled, and gripped his arm.

"You understand, old man." His voice was warm.

"Of course, Dick."

From his desk Courtney could see the mechanics preparing Scott's plane. After a delay Scott came in, stone-faced and calm.

"You wanted me, sir?"

"Sit down, Doug. I——"

"Make it quick and easy, will you? I've got a pretty good idea——"

"I don't care a damn what you've got. These are orders."

Scott shrugged and sat down. Courtney spread a map out on the desk. He pushed a fresh bottle of brandy toward Scott.

"Have a drink."

"Thanks."

They leaned over the map.

"You see the railhead here . . . and there the village . . . just a hamlet . . . the warehouse lies beside the track . . . and there," his finger touched a red circle, "is the dump."

Straightening, Courtney filled Scott's glass again. When he took his gaze from the map Scott found the drink beside him and drained it mechanically.

"About here," Courtney touched a curving black line, "you'll come over the railroad . . . you follow it south until you come to . . ."

He poured again and the amber liquor sparkled near the rim of the glass. He did not refill his own.

He talked of endless technical details . . . of instrument flying and wind-velocity effect on a curving bomb . . . of fuel supply and ammunition . . . and Scott, concentrating in his eagerness, forgot his hatred and was almost friendly again. Courtney kept filling his glass. Scott was leaning back in his chair, attentive to the voice, familiar with every delicate nuance.

"The afternoon high patrol," Courtney was saying, "will probably be back at the drome by dusk. Still, you'll have to go in low to avoid them. They might be up . . . you'll have to hit the gun, Doug . . . get in before they locate you . . . once you drop your eggs . . ."

He broke off abruptly, to find Scott watching him. For a moment there was a strained silence. Scott shattered it. He spoke impulsively, restraining his real emotion.

"Dick."

At the ring of that name on Scott's lips, Courtney looked up quickly.

"Dick, old fellow, I'm sorry . . . no end. I was a rotter. . . . I was not myself . . . when the kid went, I—I forgot everything else."

Courtney smiled and there was new happiness in his tired eyes.

"I knew, Doug. It hurt . . . at first. But I understood after a while . . . all the heaped-up things . . . no wonder you doubted me."

"But I didn't . . . not when I faced myself."

They gazed levelly into one another's eyes. Courtney said:

"Do you understand, Doug, about—Lady Mary, too? I mean, that I—I never mistrusted you and I—I want you to know that it's all right. There can't be a shadow between us."

"There isn't, Dick."

Scott gazed out at the glowing sky. He flushed and faced swiftly around.

"There's one thing," he spoke hesitantly.

"Anything at all."

Their eyes met.

"If this little jaunt goes wrong, I'd like to have you tell her. Could you do that?"

Courtney smiled curiously.

"You'd do that for me, Doug, if——"

"Of course."

Courtney nodded.

"Then it's settled." He forced a smile. "But there's a chance, Doug. Don't think——"

Scott shook his head slowly and his eyes were tranquil.

"You and I understand, fellow. There isn't a chance. But do you know," he leaned forward, "I'm not worried, somehow. Since Gordon went out, I——"

Courtney pushed the bottle toward him and touched his hand.

"Hell," he spoke gruffly, "don't go in that spirit. Have a drink. Damn it, who knows?"

They laughed nervously, each struggling to conceal his emotion. They drank a silent toast, each raising his glass to the other.

"Gordon told me about your talk with him," Scott said quietly. "It was mighty fine. He did—what you told him to do. I wish I could do as well."

Courtney pushed the bottle closer to him. He was watching a shadow from the window while Scott talked of Gordon. It lengthened slowly and at last fell across the upper half of Scott's face. He broke off frequently to drink again.

"I say, Dick," he was sprawling lazily in the chair, "when you see Mary, tell her about the kid, won't you? She thought a great deal of him."

"Indeed I shall . . . if——"

Scott lowered his chin on his breast. Courtney leaned forward over the desk and saw that his eyes were closed.

"Odd about Mary," Scott was muttering. "Always livin' up above the world . . . can't see for the life of me what she ever found in me . . . not worthy . . . no man could be, Dick. . . ."

He stirred uneasily, and reached for the glass. He drained it.

"Fact is," he rambled on, "she'll always think I was finer than I ever was . . . she'll get the wrong idea of this crazy stunt . . . you must tell her . . . it was just routine . . . foolish orders 'n' all that sort of thing. . . ."

His breath was coming heavily and his face was flushed. His lips were parted. The liquor had robbed his strong young jaws of their power of control. Beside him now, the bottle was almost empty and Courtney had taken from it sparingly.

"I was—all wrong, Dick—couldn't go without—telling you."

Courtney answered him soothingly.

"Of course, it's all right now, Doug. It's all over."

He waited for a moment and with infinite care moved the lithe body into a more comfortable position. He worked swiftly then and in

silence. In the space of a few moments he had
Scott's helmet and goggles adjusted on his own
head. He paused for one more instant and allowed his hand to rest on the wide shoulder.
Scott was fast asleep.

Courtney smiled and left him.

He moved to Bathurst's little partitioned
room and scrawled a note on a pad with pencil:

*Please report to G.H.Q. Lieutenant Scott
suffered nervous breakdown owing to death of
brother to-day. I am taking over assign-
ment.—C.*

Straightening, he went out swiftly into the
twilight. In the dusk the figures of men on the
drome were shadowy and uncertain. Courtney
moved up behind the plane and climbed into the
cockpit. Only his helmet and goggles showed
above the curving rim. None of the mechanics
recognized him. The last glow of the setting
sun painted his leather headgear a burnished
bronze, like the helmet of a knight in a dim, almost forgotten past.

He raised his hand in signal to the mechanic
at the propeller and reached for the switch.
The motor sang a rhythmic melody of power
and the ship ran out into the evening mist. . . .

In a moment it went up like a homing bird as the hour grows late, then appeared above the pines of Allonville forest, silhouetted black against the glory of the sky.

THE END

There's More to Follow!

More stories of the sort you like; more, probably, by the author of this one; more than 500 titles all told by writers of world-wide reputation, in the Authors' Alphabetical List which you will find on the *reverse side* of the wrapper of this book. Look it over before you lay it aside. There are books here you are sure to want—some, possibly, that you have *always* wanted.

It is a *selected* list; every book in it has achieved a certain measure of *success*.

The Grosset & Dunlap list is not only the greatest Index of Good Fiction available, it represents in addition a generally accepted Standard of Value. It will pay you to

Look on the Other Side of the Wrapper!

In case the wrapper is lost write to the publishers for a complete catalog

GUY FOWLER'S NOVELS

THE DAWN PATROL

In those wintry days of 1916, when England faced her doom, Richard Courtney, cynical and disilusioned, became a man of destiny, chosen for some reason to live even when he flung his challenge into the face of death.

THE SKY HAWK

The story of a chap called Bardell, a silent youngster, whose discharge from the Royal Flying Corps was not entirely honorable. The desperate chance he took to redeem himself is not on record at the British War Office but here are the facts.

THE LAST OF MRS. CHEYNEY

Based on the famous stage play by Frederic Lonsdale, this story of a beautiful adventuress and her suave, mysterious butler has charmed thousands. Here is the complete story in novel form.

FOUR DEVILS

Away from the tinsel and glamour of the arena, away from the laughter of the crowds, tragedy lurked in the lives of the daredevil troupe known as the 4 Devils. A story told from " behind the scenes."

LILAC TIME

Here is the famous story of the little french girl, Jeannine, and her love for the dashing Captain Blythe. It is one of the most beautiful romances that has come out of the war, told here in the complete novel.

GROSSET & DUNLAP, Publishers, NEW YORK

THE NOVELS OF SINCLAIR LEWIS

Within the space of a few years Sinclair Lewis has become one of the most Distinguished of American Novelists.

ELMER GANTRY

Elmer Gantry, hypocrite and voluptuary, is painted against a background of church members and professing Christians scarcely less hypocritical than he. In this book Sinclair Lewis adds a violent stroke to his growing picture of materialistic America.

MANTRAP

A clever satire on the adventures of a New York lawyer seeking rest and diversion in the northwoods. Instead of rest he finds trouble in the person of his host's wife—young, pretty and flirtatious.

ARROWSMITH

The story of a country doctor whose search for truth led him to the heights of the medical profession, to the heights and depths of love and marriage and to final peace as a quietly heroic laboratory worker in the backwoods of Vermont.

BABBITT

Every man will recognize in the character of George Babbitt, something of himself. He was a booster and a joiner, but behind all of his activities was a wistful wonder as to what life holds.

MAIN STREET

Carol Kennicott's attempt to bring life and culture to Gopher Prairie and Gopher Prairie's reaction toward her teachings have made this book one of the most famous of the last decade.

GROSSET & DUNLAP, Publishers, NEW YORK

RAFAEL SABATINI'S NOVELS

JESI, a diminutive city of the Italian Marches, was the birthplace of Rafael Sabatini.

He first went to school in Switzerland and from there to Lycee of Oporto, Portugal, and has never attended an English school. But English is hardly an adopted language for him, as he learned it from his mother, an English woman.

Today Rafael Sabatini is regarded as "The Alexandre Dumas of Modern Fiction."

THE TAVERN KNIGHT

THE NUPTIALS OF CORBAL

BELLARION

THE SHAME OF MOTLEY

THE LION'S SKIN

THE GATES OF DOOM

THE TRAMPLING OF THE LILLIES

THE STROLLING SAINT

THE CAROLINIAN

MISTRESS WILDING

THE BANNER OF THE BULL

SAINT MARTIN'S SUMMER

FORTUNE'S FOOL

BARDELY'S THE MAGNIFICENT

THE SNARE

CAPTAIN BLOOD

THE SEA-HAWK

SCARAMOUCHE

GROSSET & DUNLAP, *Publishers*, NEW YORK

THE NOVELS OF
EDGAR RICE BURROUGHS

TARZAN, LORD OF THE JUNGLE
TARZAN OF THE APES
TARZAN AND THE JEWELS OF OPAR
TARZAN AND THE ANT MEN
TARZAN AND THE GOLDEN LION
TARZAN THE TERRIBLE
TARZAN THE UNTAMED
THE BEASTS OF TARZAN
THE RETURN OF TARZAN
THE SON OF TARZAN
JUNGLE TALES OF TARZAN
THE MASTER MIND OF MARS
THE PRINCESS OF MARS
THE WARLORD OF MARS
THE GODS OF MARS
THUVIA, MAID OF MARS
THE CHESSMAN OF MARS
THE MONSTER MEN
THE WAR CHIEF
THE OUTLAW OF TORN
THE MAD KING
THE MOON MAID
THE ETERNAL LOVER
THE CAVE GIRL
THE BANDIT OF HELL'S BEND
THE LAND THAT TIME FORGOT
AT THE EARTH'S CORE
PELLUCIDAR
THE MUCKER

GROSSET & DUNLAP, *Publishers,* NEW YORK